# DEADLY OBSESSION

## DEADLIEST LOVE
### BOOK 3

## HOLLY BLOOM

DARK BLOOM PUBLISHING

*To those of you who long to be kidnapped by a hot book boyfriend. This one's for you.*

# PROLOGUE
IVY

*THAT NIGHT...*

Freddie watches as I hop into the passenger seat, clearing the empty crisp packets out of the way so I can sit down. As soon as I fasten my seatbelt, Daisy hits the accelerator. We hurtle away, rattling over the cobbles and leaving the gorgeous man I met at the bar.

"Great wing woman you are," I mutter sarcastically. We go over a speed bump, and I almost knock my head on the roof. That wasn't an accident. "Fucking hell!"

"Text me next time you go AWOL with a stranger," she snaps. "Where were you planning on going with him? What would happen if you showed up in a ditch tomorrow morning?"

Her lips purse in a judgemental line—the way they always do when she's mad, reminding me of our mum. We both look like her—the same ginger hair and freckles, but Daisy got her blue eyes with thick eyelashes, giving her a feline appearance.

"Sorry, Mum," I grumble, crossing my arms. Although

it's hard to sulk after meeting the man of my dreams. "Next time I make out with a hot guy, I'll remember to ask him if he's a serial killer first."

"He was hot," she admits reluctantly. "But did you have to give him my name, Ive?"

"I'll tell him my real name next time," I promise. Well, if Freddie was really serious about seeing me again. "Spencer knows a lot of people around here. I didn't want him to find out that I was chatting to another guy. We only broke up last week, remember?"

Daisy scowls at the mention of Spencer's name. Her knuckles turn a stark white as she tightens her grip on the wheel. She hated Spencer from the moment I introduced them. I never understood why until he showed me his true colours and became a controlling prick. I ignored the red flags, dismissing his possessiveness as being endearing, but his moods grew increasingly volatile. By the end, I didn't even recognise him anymore and when he hit me for the first time, I stopped making excuses.

"I'm glad you finally came to your senses," she says. "That rich prick never deserved you."

"If I had a drink, I'd cheers to that," I agree.

We're heading to our cottage on the Suffolk coast, three hours away. We inherited it when our parents died. While I moved to the city, Daisy made it her permanent home, and it's the perfect place for me to start rebuilding what's left of my life.

Daisy's an artist. She was in London to meet with a gallery about a potential exhibition. Since leaving Spencer, I've been flat-sitting for a friend. Earlier on, she collected the small suitcase of my belongings—the stuff Spencer hadn't destroyed.

"Nice jacket," she comments slyly. "I would have offered you my spare, but it's covered in Pippy's hair."

Daisy spends her days making art and walking the pebbled beach with Pippy, her border collie puppy with endless energy. Staying with them will give me a break from the hustle and bustle. I plan to start working freelance for a small magazine again if they'll have me back.

"I'm fine in this," I say, snuggling into Freddie's jacket. His intoxicating aftershave lingers on the fabric.

"So, who was he then?" Daisy asks. "Your tall, dark, handsome stranger?"

"Just some guy," I lie. "No one special."

She isn't buying it. "It didn't look like that when you were trying to eat his face off."

"I'll probably never hear from him again." I slip my hand into the jacket pocket to feel the sharp edges of his business card. "I need to stay single and focus on myself for a while."

Well, I'll make a start as soon as my swollen lips stop tingling.

"Are you sure you're ready to leave London?" Her brow creases in concern. "I know how much you love it here."

Although we're opposites, Daisy is my best friend. She knows me better than anyone. Am I ready to leave the place I call home? No. Do I want to leave Spencer's territory? Hell yeah. Living in his Mayfair mansion started as a dream come true until it morphed into a hellish nightmare, and its grand walls became a prison.

"It's complicated." I sigh, blowing a rogue strand of hair out of my face. "But it's the right thing to do. I won't be leaving forever."

She has an inkling about why my relationship with

Spencer fell apart, but she doesn't know all the details, and I don't want to tell her. Not yet.

"Well, you can stay with me as long as you need to," she says. "You know that."

"Thanks, Dais." I smile. "How did the meeting with the gallery go?"

"It was a waste of time," she says, ending the conversation. "You can sleep if you want. You don't have to stay awake on my account."

She turns on the radio and tunes into a Radio 4 drama that she listens to whenever she needs to unwind. That's her hint for me to shut the fuck up.

I lean my head against the cold window. I don't sleep but silently watch the bright lights disappear and think about the gorgeous man I met.

The passing landscape changes as time goes on. The motorway melds into winding country lanes, with sharper corners and fewer headlights. A layer of fog hovers over the empty fields beyond the narrow tree-lined roads, adding a layer of mystery that wouldn't look out of place in a Stephen King story.

"Jesus, Dais!" I gasp, gripping the seat and hanging on for dear life as we fly around a bend. "Are you trying to kill us?"

"Sorry," she murmurs, slowing again. The lanes are so thin that only one car can fit at a time. She checks the clock. "We're halfway home."

Somewhere along the way, my eyes flicker shut. Then, a giant force slams into the side of the car. I'm jolted awake, hoping—praying—this is still a dream, but Daisy's piercing scream makes the hairs on my neck stand.

The airbag explodes into my chest, winding me

instantly. I struggle to breathe as my ears ring from crunching metal and branches hitting the windscreen.

Everything moves in a fast, confusing blur.

We speed down a steep hill off from the road.

We're on our side and rolling.

The car tumbles, cracking with each crashing turn.

Our only working headlight illuminates a tree in our path ahead. I grab the wheel and try to swerve, but it's too late.

We don't stop.

The bonnet bends around the trunk with a sickening shriek, forcing us to a halt.

"Daisy," I croak, turning to her. She can't hear me. My chest heaves with breathing in panicked bursts. "Daisy!"

She doesn't answer. Her head hangs lifelessly. A shard of glass is wedged in a gash on her forehead. My entire body aches, but I muster all my strength to put two fingers on her neck. She has a pulse. It's slow, but it's there.

*What happened?*

*Did we hit a deer?*

*Did she take a corner too quickly?*

My instincts kick in. I shakily undo my seatbelt and brush away the tiny glass diamonds filling my lap from the shattered window. I reach for the door handle and push it open.

I have to get help.

*You can do this, Ive.*

It's now or never.

My muscles scream as I launch myself from the vehicle. It's no "Great Escape." I flop and roll through the gap with no elegance.

The ground breaks my fall. Branches tear at my knees, but I crawl and claw through the dirt. An adrenaline rush gives me the push to stagger to my feet. I'm only wearing one heel, so I kick it off. I focus on one thing: pulling Daisy from the wreckage.

I hold the car for balance and grapple my way around it, using the full moon to guide my path. When I reach the boot, the damage is apparent: a considerable dent. An animal definitely couldn't have caused it.

Through the trees, a bright, white light shines directly at me. Am I dying? My hope rises as I see the outline of a figure. *Is it him?* For a split second, I think it is. My delusion allows me to believe that Freddie will be my knight in shining armour, until…

"Bring her to me," a familiar voice orders.

My stomach drops. We won't be saved. If he's here, I'm in hell.

Four men approach. Their combat-style boots crunch through the undergrowth as they march down the hill, dressed in black SWAT-like gear.

"Help!" I scream. "My sister… She's trapped!"

They say nothing. Their faces are blank with dead eyes. I'm too weak to resist when two of them grab my shoulders. They're not taking me back to the road. Instead, they drag me deeper into the thicket of trees.

I dig the heels of my feet into the mud to leave a trail and protest. "No, you have to help her."

I try to scratch and kick; I'm too weak, and they're too strong. They throw me down like a piece of rubbish. When I look up again, I see his face twisting into a menacing snarl.

"Did you genuinely think you could leave me?" Spencer sneers. He grabs a fistful of my hair, making me howl in pain.

"You can hurt me, but help Daisy," I plead. "She's done nothing wrong. None of this is her fault!"

Over his shoulder, the other men join us, carrying a limp figure in their arms. Spencer drops his grip on me. Maybe he's going to help us after all.

"Daisy!" I yelp as they drop her carelessly. I stretch my arm, wanting to take her hand and let her know I'm here. Spencer's foot stamps down on it with force, crushing the bones in my fingers. I scream as the searing pain makes my vision swim.

"All of this is your fault, Ivy," Spencer says. "Her death will be your fault, too."

"No!" I beg, trying. "Spencer, please. I'll come back to London. I'll come back to the mansion. I'll do anything!"

He kicks me in the ribs, and I curl into a ball to protect myself as the blows keep coming. All I think of is Daisy, a few feet away, clinging to life. Please let her be okay.

"I'm only here for this one," Spencer addresses his men. "Why don't you have fun with her sister before we kill them both?"

"No!" My horrified voice echoes around the woods as a man tears the front of Daisy's dress open. "Stop it! Don't fucking touch her!"

Spencer kneels at my side. Vomit rises in my throat as he inspects my tattered jacket. Is he doing this because he found out about my drink with Freddie? Did he see us? Spencer rifles through the pockets and finds the card with Freddie's number. His face twists into a look of blazing fury. He rips the paper into tiny pieces and throws them up like confetti.

"You're mine, Ivy," he declares. "If I can't have you, no one can."

Seconds later, his fist slams into my jaw. I see stars as

he rolls me onto my stomach and climbs on top of me, using his thighs to pin me in place. Dead leaves silence me as I open my mouth to yell.

"If you want to act like a slut," he hisses, yanking my dress up to my hips, "I'll treat you like one."

He grips my hair again, forcing my head upwards at an awkward angle, then smashes my face onto the ground. My nose breaks. A gush of warmth spills down my face and leaves the bitter taste of iron in my mouth.

I try to stay awake as he pulls my knickers down, but I can't. My consciousness drifts. Everything hurts. The agony is all-consuming, and I can't tell where the pain is coming from. No matter how much my mind tries to fight it, my body can't.

I'm going to die here. Spencer will kill us both, and our bodies will never be found. My sister, the person I love more than anyone in the world, is going to die.

There's nothing I can do to stop it.

I'm powerless.

———

I was reborn again that night.

*The Killers Club gave me power. They turned me into a brutal killing machine and severed me from my emotions.*

*The promise of revenge has kept my heart beating for the last five years, but how far will I go to get what I want, and who will I have to kill to get it?*

# CHAPTER 1

IVY



"We need to go," Stephanie hisses in my ear. "Now."

She grabs my hand and almost dislocates my shoulder as she yanks me in the opposite direction to the hysterical screams ringing through the night air.

Screams I caused.

I knew Callen's gift to Lord McGowan wouldn't be a teddy bear or a box of chocolates, but a bomb? That bastard knows how to make a statement and owes me big time.

Alaric stops to watch the flames consuming the manor with a thunderous expression. The interior wooden panelling helped the inferno spread, and the entire building is quickly turning into a bonfire. The blaze has thwarted his plans of killing Seb, and he's torn, weighing up the risks of returning to finish the job.

"Come on, Ric," Stephanie insists firmly, reading his mind. "We need to go before the authorities arrive."

Seb may get away, but he knows she's right. Uninvited guests being discovered at a bombsite would fall under immediate suspicion.

He scowls. "Fine."

Screeching sirens wail in the distance, growing closer, but we have time to escape. One advantage of Collingsbrook Manor being secluded is the delayed emergency response time.

"How did you know where to find me?" I ask as we quicken our pace.

"We'll talk later," Alaric snaps in a steely tone that'd make hell freeze over. As well as his murderous rampage being nipped in the bud, it sounds like he's preparing to give me a lecture. "Just keep fucking moving."

"This way." Stephanie points to a hedge at the edge of the rose garden. Of course, they found another entrance. "Over it."

I raise my eyebrows and swish the skirt of my black ballgown. "Have you seen my dress?"

"Not funny, Ivy," she warns. "Climb. Now."

I scale the hedge, tearing the delicate layers of expensive fabric as I manage to land on the other side without falling. Cinderella didn't have to deal with this shit.

The narrow country lane is deserted, aside from our Jeep, and there are no cameras in sight. Next to the road, a security guard's feet poke out from beneath a hedge row where they temporarily stashed his body. Alaric grabs his ankles and heaves him out. A walkie-talkie balances on the dead man's chest. Panicked voices crackle over the line, strategizing like headless chickens about where to position themselves.

"Position four," a voice cuts through the chaos. "Can you copy?"

The number four is stuck on the back of the walkie-talkie. We made it here at the perfect time.

Alaric picks up and answers, "Nothing unusual here. The road is empty. No one is getting in or out this way."

Hiring a private firm for a function has downsides since many guards are employed specially for the occasion. None of them notices one of their team has been swapped for an assassin.

"What're you both standing around for?" Alaric barks at us as the voice continues to do a roll call. "Get in the car!"

I clamber into the back seat.

"Shame you didn't bring a horse and carriage," I murmur sarcastically.

The front doors slam as the other two get in. Their conspicuous judgemental glares sear into me through the rearview mirror. They're studying my reaction and searching for weaknesses. I bring a wall down over my emotions to collect myself, pushing aside visions of Seb being caught in the blast.

"We're on the move, Penelope," Alaric says into his earpiece. "Which route should I take?"

He pauses to listen to her brief response, then he floors it.

"I could sue you for whiplash," I mumble, massaging my chest.

He ignores me, switching on the radio to tune into the police and ambulance services to avoid any nasty surprise encounters while he continues to follow Penelope's directions for the best escape route.

Over the hedges, smoke billows into the starry sky. At least Graham will get a free cremation—hopefully, he'll be charred enough that the coroner won't be able to discern his actual cause of death.

"If you keep following this road and the signs back to London, you're in the clear," Penelope says. "I'll keep monitoring your route for any changes."

"I'll call you back if we need anything else," he replies gruffly.

*BOOM!*

I spin my head to look through the back window at what we've left behind. We have a better vantage point from our elevated position, and an explosion illuminates the sky with an orange glow. Years of history turn to ash in an instant, just like my connection to the Dukes.

Stephanie laughs. "Talk about ending the night with a bang..."

"Why don't you enlighten us, Ivy?" Alaric says with zero humour. His eyes narrow in the rearview mirror, paying more attention to me than the road. "What happened tonight?"

He's doing more than the national speed limit through the bendy lanes, and I resist the urge to tell him to slow down. That'd be more dangerous than pouring petrol over the Collingsbrook fire.

I make a snap decision. "Faulty wiring, I guess." I shrug and keep my voice light-hearted. He'll see through my inflexions if I'm not convincing enough. "Did you see the building? It was so old, I'm surprised it was still standing."

"And the Dukes had nothing to do with it?"

"They could have," I reply, "but if they did, they didn't tell me about it."

"Faulty wiring..." he repeats, unconvinced. "If you say so."

I can't lose my nerve. If he knew I was involved, he'd think I'm a compromised agent, and I'm not. Am I?

"What was your plan, Ivy?" Stephanie's usually friendly tone is replaced by the voice of the emotionless killer that everyone fears. She's speaking to me like a target, not a friend she's known for years. "We know who the Dukes are. Your mission was clear. You had three days. How much longer were you going to let them live? We wanted bodies, not ballgowns."

If I give the wrong answer, they won't take me back to HQ. They'll leave me to die in a ditch, just like Spencer. There'd be a poetic irony to it, considering that's where my journey with the Killers Club started.

"Tom ruined everything," I declare. "If he hadn't barged in unannounced, I would have stayed on track. The Dukes had to pivot and took me to a safe house in the middle of nowhere. I've been earning their trust."

Stephanie straightens in her seat, and her pouty lips press into a thin line—a micro-movement that tells me they haven't found Tom's body yet, even though they have suspicions about what happened.

"What did they do with Tom's body?"

"Funnily enough, they didn't show me where they buried it," I say. "You know, with me pretending to be a journalist and all."

"Enough with the sarcasm." Alaric chastises me like I'm a naughty school child. "Where's their safe house?"

"Erm…" I take a deep breath. "About that…"

Stephanie's pretty pout vanishes as she purses her lips, making deeper lines appear on either side of her mouth. Maybe she's had to miss a Botox session because of all the stress. "You don't know?"

My anger rises. They're treating me like an amateur. Haven't I proved myself over the years?

"They blindfolded me for my protection," I explain.

"What information *do* you have about them?" Stephanie sneers. "Or were you too busy screwing your new boyfriend to get any information?"

Heat creeps up my neck, and butterflies flutter in my stomach, though I don't let my nerves show.

"They have a secret room on the top floor of their London house," I say, choosing to ignore her diggy remark. "It's filled with weapons and enough ammunition to sink half the capital. Thanks to Tom's interruption, I didn't have long to look around, but they're better connected than we thought."

"Interesting," Alaric ponders. His eyebrows crease as he takes that in, and his stiff jaw softens slightly. He'll be questioning how they acquired such a sizable supply and who they bought it from.

"Freddie used to be an arms dealer in Italy," I explain. "Something happened to his family there. That's where he'll be getting the weapons from. He'll have contacts."

"What about the other two?" Stephanie asks. "Sebastian and Callen. How do they fit into the Dukes' operation?"

Stephanie may as well be shining a light into my face in an interrogation room. She takes her job seriously, but she needs to back off.

"Callen used to be a surgeon, but he's a total psychopath. He's their wild card, and someone to watch out for," I say. "Seb's their networker. He knows people in all the right places and helps with funding. Callen and Freddie use shadow companies to hide their dealings, including a private security firm, but all Seb's business is legitimate."

"Smart, but not smart enough," Stephanie comments. "It's a shame we'll have to kill them all, especially Seb. You know I'm a sucker for guys with dimples."

I breathe a sigh of relief at her normal bubbly personality returning. Maybe they won't kill me after all.

"The Dukes have killed two of our agents!" Alaric slams the steering wheel with his fists. "They won't get away with it."

"Patience, my love." Stephanie places a perfectly manicured hand on his forearm to calm him and stop us from crashing. "All in good time."

"So, what did I miss at HQ?" I ask. It's been less than a week, but it already feels like a lifetime. "I heard the Lotus is back in the city—the Dukes were talking about Doyle Jackson's death, and I recognised her signature. When can I meet her?"

"You know the rules," Stephanie says. She flips the sun visor down and uses the compact mirror to touch up her pink lip gloss. "It's safer for everyone if we don't know each other's identities."

It's a rule I've never agreed with. What if we accidentally killed each other? There are other Killers Club buildings dotted across the globe where other agents live, but Alaric keeps us isolated in 'pods' of five or six.

"It's unfortunate that the rest of your pod are dead or in the hospital," Alaric says. "I can't decide whether that's an ill-fated coincidence or if you're the problem."

Or perhaps I had the doomed luck of being grouped with incompetent imbeciles. The Tweedles killed themselves by walking into bullets and not following the rules.

Jonathon's better at his job, but I'm not to blame for his inability to beat Bram in a fight.

"I've never let you down. And I don't plan on starting now. I would have killed the Dukes if I had more time." I decide to change the subject, steering it away from less rocky waters. "How is Jonathon?"

"He can open his eyes and sip a drink through a straw, so it's an improvement," Stephanie says dismissively, now touching up her bronzer. "He'll be fine."

"Good." The guy survived getting his throat slashed, so this is nothing in comparison. "And what about our prisoner?"

Although I don't care what happens to Bram, I saw how much he meant to Seb and Freddie. His death would crush them.

"He's still alive and kicking," Stephanie says. "For now."

For some reason, knowing that makes my chest feel lighter. It's been a long night. Inhaling the smoke from the fire must be messing with my head.

"It's good to have you back, Ivy," Alaric says in a glacial tone.

He grins, but it looks more like a grimace, putting me on edge. I'm not forgiven yet.

"It's good to be back," I reply, forcing a smile.

I left destruction in my wake, but I might be heading into something far worse…

# CHAPTER 2
## SEB

I splutter as acrid smoke assaults my lungs. The rising smog makes it hard to see, and the heat from the flames burns my cheeks as it devours a manor that's been a British institution for years. Watching it burn would be a beautiful sight if the woman I love wasn't trapped inside.

"Rose," I rasp. My throat is hoarse from how many times I've screamed her name. "Rose!"

She doesn't answer.

Other guests tried to drag bodies out of the smoke but ended up leaving them behind because they were too afraid of ending up like them. Five men lie dead around Lord Callahan. There's no sign of my beauty in a ballgown.

I shield my face from the falling debris. There's a bang at the end of the corridor. The walls look like they're shaking as flames lick up their sides.

*Where is she?*

*Why didn't I follow her?*

Fuck! I don't know why I thought bringing her here

was a good idea. Selfishly, I wanted to introduce her to my family and bring her into my world, but I should have known better.

I peel off my suit jacket and hold it over my head as I trudge closer to the flames, pushing against all of my instincts telling me to run. I won't leave without her. Walking is like wading through quicksand. I struggle to keep my watery eyes open.

"Sebastian!" My mother's screech rings over the rest of the crowd. "Somebody stop him!"

I don't listen. I jump out of the way to avoid being hit by a part of the ceiling falling at my feet in a fiery clump, warning me to stay back. An almighty crack from above hints that the entire floor is going to cave. The flames are spreading, creating a wall of heat.

Strong arms grab my shoulders and heave me backwards.

"Have you got a death wish?" my brother, Ralph, hisses in my ear as his fingers dig into my skin and haul me away. "Mum nearly had a heart attack."

I shrug him off, but we get pushed along with another crowd and swept outside. Sirens grow closer, and three fire engines pull up. The men burst from its doors and hurry to get their hoses ready to fight the blaze.

Lord and Lady Collingsbrook are weeping. "Please God, save our home!"

Praying won't help. The damage has already been done. A building this old will never recover.

"My girlfriend's in there!" I scream desperately as one of them rushes past. He doesn't listen.

At the bottom of the steps, the entire party has assembled in the garden. Women are crying, their previously pristine make-up streaks down their cheeks. Some men are even missing shoes. At the end of the drive, my cousin is being whisked back to Buckingham Palace.

"Sebastian!" Mum rushes forward. Her voice is more high-pitched than usual, but she's not concerned. No, I can detect her overwhelming disappointment a mile away. "What on earth were you thinking?"

"I don't have time for this," I say, pushing past her.

"Sebastian!" A weeping Beatrice latches onto my arm as I try to get away. "Daddy, he's… he's…"

"It's okay, dear." Mum hurries over and puts a protective arm around her. She's never shown me that kind of motherly love before. It's all to keep up appearances. "Come over here and sit with me."

"But… Seb…" Beatrice whimpers, but I have no time for her crocodile tears. No one liked her father, and I'm betting she didn't either.

"You should stay with Beatrice, Sebastian," Mum orders.

I draw myself up to full height. I'm not a toddler that she can boss around anymore.

"Didn't you hear me the first time?" I hiss venomously, making her eyes boggle in outrage. "Rose is still inside!"

If she were here, I'd tell her that everything would be okay and hold onto her tightly. I feel like I've been pushed off a cliff, but half of my body has been left behind. Is this how Freddie felt for the last five years?

Mum casts a worried glance over her shoulder and hisses, "Stop making a scene. Pull yourself together, Sebastian!"

How can I when Rose is missing? I half expect her to run and jump into my arms at any moment, but she doesn't.

The panic is overwhelming as the fire crew makes their way inside, and I hear snippets of conversations.

"What happened?"

"Was it a bomb?"

"It could have been an assassination attempt on the prince!"

Spencer's distinct voice drawls over the others, boasting about saving someone from being squashed by a falling animal head. The only thing he saved was his own arse.

I wipe my eyes with my dusty jacket sleeve. "Rose…"

The fire crew pulls bodies from the wreckage, ready to put them into the row of waiting ambulances. I race towards them, needing to know, needing to check that Rose isn't among them.

"You need to stand back," a paramedic says, but I ignore him and peer at the face of a heavily burned man who I recognise as someone my father played chess with.

Then there's a woman on a stretcher heading in our direction…

I ignore their calls for me to stay back like an animal possessed. I need Rose. I need to see she's okay to get rid of the dread trying to tear my chest open because I can't live without her. Losing her would destroy me.

The injured woman is wearing a black dress, but I can't see her properly. The police are putting up yellow tape to block off the scene, and I leap over it like a hurdle, but I don't get far.

A burly security officer—the same arsehole who was monitoring the gate at the start of the night—tries to tackle me to the ground. I swing a punch and break his nose.

The onlookers scream, but I don't care what they think. I step over his bleeding body, and a police officer lunges to take me down. Adrenaline takes over, and I smash my fist into his face too. I'll take on anyone who stands in my way.

It takes three of them to restrain me. All of them are bloody and bruised by the time I'm done. Out of the corner of my eye, I get a proper look at the woman and see a strand of blonde hair trailing off the stretcher. It's not Rose.

I'm hauled roughly to my feet, and they thrust my wrists into handcuffs.

"Sebastian Montgomery," an officer with a split lip says, "you are under arrest."

Cameras flash in my direction. It's not the paparazzi taking photos, but the party guests. If a fire at the Collingsbrook Ball isn't enough of a scandal, my arrest will be…

# CHAPTER 3

## CALLEN

Finally, it's done. Justice has been served. The man who killed my baby is dead, even if his death won't bring Tilly back.

I can't stop grinning as I watch the scene unfolding at the manor.

"Holy shit…"

My mouth falls open at what I'm seeing. If watching Lord Callahan getting blown to pieces didn't make tonight extra special, seeing Seb lose control in front of the toffs he's spent years trying to impress is the cherry on top of the cake.

I check my watch to see how much time I have. If I left when Freddie told me to, I'd still be on the road. I have time to kill; all I'm missing now is popcorn for the show.

Amidst the chaos, Seb roars and dives over the police line. He throws a punch at anyone who stands in his way and sheds his suit jacket. Usually, Seb is all about manners and decorum. Who knew the lad had it in him? Seb's the youngest of the Dukes. His boyish humour often makes him appear younger than he is, but right now, he's grown a pair of massive bollocks.

"Go on, Seb. Let him have it," I encourage as he swings for the officer. If I was there, I'd dive in and join them, but I don't have the connections to erase a scandal. If I touched anyone, I'd get locked up for years, while Seb would only get a slap on the wrist. He lands the punch, smacking into his opponent's jawline. "Nice."

It's a shame all of his actions are for nothing, and he's only going to get his heart broken. How will he react when he discovers Rose isn't who he thinks she is and that she never needed his protection? She isn't helpless and innocent; she's a Killers Club agent who's been sent to murder us. She could have known Seb was a Duke all along, and it might have been no accident she ran into him that night.

Rose and her friends have already made their getaway through the garden. Their car disappeared in the opposite direction, allowing Rose to slink back under the radar while Seb risks everything for someone he thinks he loves.

Rose—Daisy, whoever the fuck she is—walked into our lives and changed everything. Now that she's completed the job for me, I have no reason not to kill her—unless I want to fuck her incredibly tight pussy again.

I shake my head, watching Seb fight against the officers trying to wrangle him into cuffs. "Bad luck, kid."

I take a few pictures on my phone—they'll cheer me up when I'm having a bad day. Maybe I'll even get them printed on a calendar or mug to commemorate the occasion.

It's time to call Freddie to let him know what's going on.

"Well?" Freddie answers on the second ring. He's still

driving, and the engine roars in the background as he speeds along the motorway. "Have you found them?"

"About that…" I pause dramatically. "We've stumbled into a problem."

"What kind of problem?"

"Where do I start?" I'm unable to keep the glee out of my voice. "Collingsbrook Manor went up in flames, your golden boy is currently being put into the back of a police car, and Rose…"

"What about her?"

"She's gone."

"Gone?" He ignores everything else I've said, fixating on the woman who is his obsession. She's hypnotised them, giving Freddie and Seb tunnel vision and rendering their other skills useless. Maybe that's why the Killers Club wanted her. A woman who can enchant men with magical pussy powers. "Where is she?"

"I don't know," I lie, deciding to postpone telling him about the true nature of her betrayal. "I can't see her anywhere. People are leaving, so she could have got into a car with someone else."

"Fuck!" Freddie yells, then quickly regains his authoritative stance. "Follow Seb to the station. His mother will have their family lawyer on speed dial, but he'll need someone to pick him up when he's done. She won't let a Montgomery stay in a cell overnight."

"I'm on it," I say, slinging one leg over my bike. "And don't worry about Rose, boss." A sly grin crosses my face. "We'll find her."

I've always liked games, and Rose might be the best game I've played yet.

# CHAPTER 4

## BRAM

They're back.

I jump to my feet. My empty stomach gurgles at the smell of Chinese food wafting down the corridor. I've begrudgingly eaten the scraps they've put in front of me for days, but this smells heavenly, and I'm already salivating like one of Pavlov's dogs. This isn't good. If they're bringing food, they either want to torture me or bargain.

"I'm here to talk, Bram."

Alaric's footsteps draw closer. He's alone, which is unusual. From what I've seen, he usually moves with an entourage in tow. Keys clatter on the other side of the door, and he pushes my cell door open.

"Don't do anything stupid," he warns, placing the bag of food on the floor and tapping the gun in his holster.

I'm too weak to win a fight, even if I wanted to. The light flickers ominously in the corridor. Is this like a death row inmate getting their favourite meal before being put out of their misery?

He unpacks the food carefully. There's more than

enough in the plastic cartons for two people, but I don't move.

"You might be wondering why I'm here," he begins.

*No fucking shit.* I narrow my eyes. *How can I be sure the food isn't poisoned?*

"I'm not trying to kill you," he says, reading my mind.

Death by chow mein wouldn't be the worst way to go. I approach cautiously, shuffling across the cold floor to grab the nearest warm box and a pair of chopsticks. Alaric does the same.

I wait until he's taken his first mouthful to begin. It's plausible he may not have poisoned his food, but I'm too hungry to give a shit or over-analyse. *Fuck the chopsticks.* I abandon them and pick up the noodles with my hands, being careful not to choke by eating too fast. With a large part of my tongue missing, eating takes more effort and I have to take it easy.

We eat in silence, reminding me of my time in Iraq. A particular memory comes to mind. After an intense day in the field, we took a moment of stillness in the desert at night. Despite the earlier bloodshed, I remember looking up at the stars. They were the most beautiful I'd ever seen. It's one of the few fond memories I have of my time overseas. Like now, it was a moment of calm in the middle of the storm.

When I was a rookie on my first tour, Alaric was a Lieutenant, but I never saw him until the night I brought Ivy to him. As a soldier, he'd cultivated a ruthless reputation through his ability to make men follow him blindly. Loyalty, dedication, and commitment were everything to him—values he instilled in his Killers Club agents.

"You were a good soldier, Bram," he says, slurping a

mouthful of noodles. "Who thought it'd have come to this?"

I ignore him, savouring the delicious hint of sesame oil, the sweet sauce, and the umami undertones. This may be the best meal I've ever tasted.

"Here." Alaric rolls a can of Coke across the floor. "You'll need this to wash it down." He pulls a packet of custard creams out of his jacket pocket. "I got you these for later."

I drop my chopsticks. My biscuit addiction isn't a new thing, and the fucker remembered. I narrow my eyes. *What do you want?* I won't eat another morsel until I know what he's planning.

"Come on, don't be like that," he teases. "Your food will go cold."

My jaw hardens. *You better start fucking talking, or else.* I won't be manipulated, no matter how good the meal tastes. *Get to the point.*

"Fine!" He holds up his hands. "I have a proposition."

I grunt. *What can I offer you?*

"You're talented, Bram. You always have been. I recognised it in the army, and I recognise it now," he says. "We could use someone around here with your skills. It took our technical team a few days to get past some of your security measures, which I've never seen happen before."

*Do I look like a crumpet?* He's buttering me up, and his attempts at flattery won't work. Compliments don't detract from how he's holding me prisoner, running an operation that revolves around deception and turning innocent people into cold-blooded killers. After what happened to Ivy, how can I trust anything that comes from his lying, good-for-nothing mouth?

"Why should you trust the man who cut out your

tongue?" He vocalises my thoughts aloud. "I get it. We have a history, but you understand why I did it. It was a business decision, purely for her protection."

If I'd known what he'd planned to turn her into, I'd never have sought his help. After leaving the army, I got a job in security and ended up as a driver for Spencer Bexley. A week before Spencer tried to kill Ivy, I met with an old friend who told me about Alaric's private witness protection operation. No one knew the truth.

"I'll give you more power than the Dukes can," Alaric says. "They're a bunch of unsophisticated criminals. They're small fry. You're made for bigger things. The Killers Club can give you everything you've ever wanted. I want you to join us."

I crack open the Coke with a pop and slug it. The sugary drink and his words make me uneasy. Is this the same speech he used on Ivy and the others he recruited? I tilt my head to the side, wanting him to elaborate. The more he talks, the better my chance of working out his true intentions.

"I'll level with you," he says, trying to give the illusion that we're friends. "I don't want to keep you down here, tethered like a dog. There's a place waiting for you upstairs, but I'll need your word."

I open my mouth to make a point. *Giving my word would be easier if you hadn't cut out my fucking tongue.*

"Still a sarcastic fucker, huh?" He chuckles. "Nod your head if you're interested."

I take a long pause, and his eyes lock on mine. Nothing is hiding behind them. He's barely human. He doesn't care about his agents, contrary to how he acts. All he wants is control. Getting people to kill for you is the ultimate act of

God. But this lifeline he's giving me could be the only way to survive.

I wipe my mouth on the back of my hand, then nod curtly.

"Good." Alaric smiles, sliding the custard creams across the floor like he's giving his pet dog a treat for good behaviour. "But I need you to prove you're serious. If you want to join us, I need something from you in return."

Pet or not, I grab the custard creams before he can take them back and gesture for him to keep talking.

"Ivy has been gallivanting with your old friends," he says. My ears prick up. "I need you to test Ivy's loyalty."

I scoff. She seemed pretty loyal when she was ripping my fingernails off.

"I'll give you the combination to your cell door. If you can talk Ivy into opening it, she fails the test," he says. "She'll be watching you for the next few weeks, trying to get information out of you. That's all the time you'll have." He reaches into the takeaway bag and retrieves a notebook and pen stashed in the bottom of it. "You'll communicate with her in writing."

I pick them up and write:

*What happens if she doesn't open the door?*

"Then I have nothing to worry about," he replies. "Life continues as normal."

*And if she opens the door?*

"That's not something to concern yourself with." He

grins menacingly. "But if you don't try your best, we'll have a problem."

*What will happen to the Dukes?*

"To show you my generosity, I'll let the Dukes live for now. If you follow through with our deal and join us, I'll negotiate with them," he says. "I'll give them a chance to leave the country unless they want to die an excruciating death at the hands of our newest agent." His eyes glitter. "I haven't forgotten what you're capable of."

I'd rather die than join the Killers Club, but I can buy the Dukes more time.

Alaric stands and brushes himself off. "Do we have ourselves a deal?"

I nod. *Well, for now…*

# CHAPTER 5

IVY

Killers Club HQ is the opposite of the Dukes' kitschy cottage. I gaze through the window into the starkly lit medical room where Jonathon is sleeping. Bandages are wrapped around his head, and Ash and the Basilisk's music blares in the background.

"It's an odd choice of a lullaby, right?" Stephanie creeps up behind me from out of nowhere, making me jump. Her outfit choice is fitting: a skin-tight black shiny jumpsuit that makes her look like a spy.

"If anyone's voice will heal him, it'll be Ash's," I say confidently. "She has the perfect scream."

I make a mental note to buy Jonathon a ticket to see them when he recovers. After Ash had a baby, the band took a break, but rumour has it, they're getting ready to do a comeback world tour. Having Ash as a mum and hot masked dads must be the coolest—although Jonathon went into mourning after her pregnancy announcement. He couldn't handle the thought of her fucking someone other than him in his dreams.

"How are you adjusting?" she asks.

I'm not sure whether she's asking as my friend or superior. Since day one, Stephanie has had my back, but her loyalty to Alaric supersedes all else. Even if I wanted to, I couldn't tell her what happened during my time with the Dukes. I can't trust her, or anyone else, within these walls —especially after seeing how she reacted at the manor.

"Fine, but I'm… frustrated." I blow a loose strand of hair out of my face. "I didn't want to let the club down."

If she's going to run back to Alaric to tell him everything I say, I want to make damn sure I'm saying the right things. The reality is, adjusting has been more challenging than expected. I've always felt at home at HQ, but since returning, I've become extra vigilant and can't shake the feeling that something bad is going to happen.

"You'll make it up to us," she says, wrapping her arm around my shoulder and squeezing it tightly. "You're Ivy-fucking-Penrose. One of our very best."

Praise like that used to make me burst with pride, but her words don't hit in the same way anymore. What's wrong with me?

I fake a smile. "How mad is Alaric?"

"He'll get over it." She shrugs. "The Dukes are going to die soon enough."

"Is he going after them now?" I ask, ignoring the creeping dread bubbling in my stomach.

I shouldn't care about our marks and what happens to them. I can't!

"Not yet," she replies, smoothing down her waist-length blonde hair. "We'll give them some time to regroup, and then we'll let them come to us. It'll be an excellent test of our security measures."

Every few years, a gang gets caught up in the Killers

Club's operations. Some of them even try to track us down, but none of them succeed.

"So, Frederick James…" she says. Her watchful stare scorches the side of my face, and I imagine a wrinkly eighty-year-old with balls that hang down to his ankles to distract me from thinking about Freddie. "How do you know him? He seemed very keen to protect you at the restaurant."

Lying comes easily. "We knew each other years ago. We went on one date, and that was it." Again, I use my principle of basing a lie on the truth to make it more convincing. "I completely forgot about it until I saw him again at the bar."

"That one date must have made quite an impression on him," she says. "Not many men would jump in front of a bullet for a woman he hardly knows."

"He's old-fashioned," I say. "He likes to play the saviour and be a knight in shining armour. Macho bullshit."

"He could be my saviour any day." She nudges me in the ribs jokily. Her shoulders relax, like I've passed her test and signal that she's out of work mode now, but I can't let my guard down. "The guy is smoking hot."

"You better make sure Alaric doesn't hear you say that."

"So, what happened between you?" she asks, wiggling her eyebrows. "Did he and Seb fight over you?"

*Think of shrivelled wrinkly balls, Ivy!*

"It's real life, not a why choose romance novel," I say. "They thought I was a journalist and just wanted to keep me safe. Protecting people is what they do."

"Boring!" she cries in a sing-song voice. "Who would

you rather fuck? Freddie, the Italian stallion, or Seb, the pretty prince?"

*Both* my inner voice answers immediately, *preferably together*. I think of the most unsexy things I can: dirty fingernails, pus-oozing penises, and shit-stained underwear… anything that stops my mind from straying to what happened in front of the fireplace the night Freddie and Seb gave me the most pleasure I've ever experienced.

"Seb," I answer, sticking to the safer choice. She already knows we slept together. "I wouldn't have ever gone on a date with him if I knew who he was."

"You slept with him again, didn't you?"

"What choice did I have?" I say. "I had to keep my cover."

"Don't tell Alaric, but…" She looks over her shoulder to check we're alone. "There's something hot about fucking someone you're about to kill, right? I'm not saying sex with Alaric isn't incredible, because it is, but knowing you're going to end the life of someone you're screwing is the biggest power trip. I swear everyone should try it. It makes my orgasms ten times more intense."

Has Stephanie always been this fucking crazy? A few days with the Dukes has messed with my head somehow, making me see everything with a different perspective. All of this is their fault! They made me feel something for the first time in years. Emotions I didn't think I was capable of, and now I'm questioning things I shouldn't.

"You're unbelievable." I roll my eyes, keeping it light-hearted. "That's why you're the best honey trap."

She flicks her hair over her shoulder and flashes me her perfect, dazzling smile like a shark before it rips apart its prey. "I know."

Alaric steps from the shadows, phasing out of nothingness. "What're you talking about?"

"Nothing for you to worry about." Stephanie winks. "Just girl talk."

I need to snap out of whatever weird headspace I'm in before I destroy my entire life. I'm an assassin, and if I don't start acting like it, I'll be the one with a bullet between my eyes...

# CHAPTER 6

## SEB

The holding cell has a sink, toilet, and uncomfortable rock-hard bed—a far cry from my usual surroundings. I've not been able to sit still and haven't washed the blood from my knuckles yet. I can't think straight in a space this small.

Suddenly, the door opens, and a man with no chin and an ill-fitting shirt fills the entire frame. The officer looks down his nose at me like he wants to spit at my feet. I don't blame him. I have the same visceral reaction when seeing other rich men acting like arseholes.

"You're free to go," he grunts.

I've been held for less than an hour. I hate my toxic family and their crippling expectations, but admittedly, there are some perks to being royal and having a lawyer on retainer.

I straighten the collar of my blood and dirt-streaked white shirt. My entire body aches, and my limbs feel three times heavier. Red rings circle my wrists from the handcuffs. I didn't notice they were fastened so tightly because Rose is all that's occupying my thoughts. She's all I see.

"Thanks, officer," I mumble.

He scowls in reply and nudges his head, gesturing for me to follow. He leads me through the bleak corridors of the police station. Behind other doors, prisoners yell and swear. Most of them are rowdy drunks.

At the front desk, my brother is standing ramrod-straight. His nose is scrunched up like he's smelling something unpleasant. Unlike mine, his navy suit has remained almost immaculate despite escaping the blaze. That's typical of Ralph; he never wants to get his hands dirty.

"There you are," he says, marching over to me. "Mother is furious."

I laugh in his face. When the laughter comes, I can't stop it. It grows hysterical, echoing and drawing attention to us. The nearby receptionist shifts uncomfortably in her seat and a nearby officer's hand jumps to his baton.

"What're you doing?" Ralph hisses. Red blotches appear over his neck, giving him a Dalmatian-like complexion. "Pull yourself together, Sebastian! If Mother hears about—"

"Do you honestly think I care about what Mother thinks?" I interrupt.

I step closer, and Ralph winces. If I'm not afraid of taking on the police, think of what damage I could do to Mummy's golden boy.

"I don't know what's going on with you." He uses the hoity-toity tone he reserves for functions when he meets people less fortunate than himself. "Do you need professional help?" He swallows hard. "Do we need to talk about rehab?"

"Rehab?" That sets my laughter off again. A tear slides down my face, and I wipe it away with my grubby finger before composing myself. My face returns to a deadpan expression. "There's nothing wrong with me, but I'm not the one who needs help." I look him up and down. "You and the family are more bothered about me making a scene than the fact people died tonight. God forbid our precious fucking family comes under scrutiny! Who cares if they splash our names all over the tabloids? Some things are more important than the institution."

He gasps as if I've told him Buckingham Palace will be turned into the Playboy Mansion. His expression darkens. He grabs my arm in a vice-like grip and drags me across to the exit, smiling apologetically over his shoulder to the staff, who are watching our altercation curiously. The chilly breeze stings my open wounds and ripples through my clothes to spread the smell of smoke that still clings to them.

"What the fuck are you doing?" Ralph demands. "If people heard you talking like that, they could—"

"They could, what?" I spit. "Who cares what they think?"

"You need to think of the family," he says. "Don't you understand how much time we're going to have to spend on damage control? Pictures of you could be front-page news tomorrow."

"So?" I say. "If me getting arrested is more important than people dying, then I question the country we live in."

For a second, I thought I saw a flicker of understanding stir behind his eyes. As the oldest brother, Ralph faced more pressure than most, but he was always keen to fulfil his responsibilities. That look vanishes and gives way to fury.

"Never let anyone else hear you say that," he snarls. "You may not want this life, but you have no choice."

"I'm not like you," I say. "I'm not a cog in this fucking machine. Can't you see how wrong this is? People died."

"And you are royal." His eyes narrow. "You have a duty to this country."

"I'm not the next in line for the throne!" I say. "And whatever happens, you can't drain the blood from my fucking veins, no matter how much Mother wants to."

"You can't change who you are, Sebastian."

I ignore him and ask about what's really on my mind. "Have you heard from Rose?"

"Rose?" Ralph knows exactly who I'm talking about, but he'd prefer to pretend she doesn't exist because she doesn't fit into our family's idea of perfection.

I clench my fists, resisting the urge to punch him and get thrown straight back into the hole.

Across the car park, a growling motorbike roars towards us, making Ralph jump back like he's terrified that being within a few inches of it will knock him a few rungs down the social class ladder.

The Harley comes to a stop in front of us. Callen pulls off his helmet and shakes his hair. He grins at me. "I thought you might need a ride."

Ralph's lip curls in disapproval as he takes in Callen's long locks, beard, and his tattoos over his knuckles. He's someone Ralph would usually call security to remove at an event.

"Sebastian, you need to come with me," Ralph says, but his voice is a few octaves higher, like someone is holding his balls in a lemon squeezer. "You need to be with the family. Mother will be furious if—"

"If you love your mother so much, why don't you go back and fuck her?" Callen suggests, finishing his sentence.

He's joking, but Ralph gasps in horror as his cheeks turn beet red. "You're repulsive!"

Callen turns back to me and taps an imaginary watch on his wrist. "Come on, we don't have all night."

He holds out a helmet.

"Sebastian!" Ralph objects as I take it. "I strongly insist that you come with me. Mother will—"

"Fuck you, Ralph," I end the conversation.

Callen's revving bike silences any more arguments. Being pressed up against Callen isn't how I imagined my evening ending, but it beats being around my family. Although, returning to my second family won't be any easier. When I return to the safe house, Freddie will want to know what happened to Rose…

# CHAPTER 7
## FREDDIE

They'll be back soon.

I walk around the cottage. Back and forth. Room to room. Carpet to wooden floors. The eyes of the young royals hanging in frames watch and taunt me. I clench my fists, fighting my instincts to hurl them from their hooks, tear the cottage apart, and smash everything in grabbing range.

Callen's words still ring in my head, blaring through my brain like an air-raid siren.

*Rose is gone.*

On my way to the safe house, I passed a road leading to Collingsbrook Manor. It was crawling with police, sections of the route cordoned off, and overhead helicopters swept the area. I couldn't get close enough to the scene to search for Rose, even if I tried.

Gravel crunching in the driveway makes me hurry to the window to see Seb staggering off Callen's bike. He looks like he's been through a plane crash. His suit is in tatters, his shirt ripped like a pirate's, his knuckles are bloody, and his skin is covered in soot.

He catches me staring. Our eyes meet. *You were supposed to look after her.* He hangs his head in shame, feeling the full force of my unsaid accusation shooting through the air and slicing his skin. *I trusted you.*

My questions about the photograph of Rose and Spencer vanish as the door slams behind them. My fear of losing her again overpowers my logical reasoning. It transports me back to that night five years ago. A night when I stayed awake waiting for a call that never came. A night when I wanted to hear she was safe. A night that changed everything and left me with no one to blame. Rose disappeared without a trace then, but this is different... it's Seb's fault.

As soon as Seb enters the kitchen, I grab him by the scruff of his collar and smash his back into the wall. He doesn't try to resist.

"Where is she?" I demand through gritted teeth. Adrenaline and fury sear through my veins. I've not felt anger like this since I returned to find my family dead in our Italian villa.

I trusted Seb to take care of her. That was a mistake. I shouldn't have trusted anyone but myself. Doesn't he understand how special she is?

"Freddie," Seb stammers, struggling to breathe as I cut off his airway. His green eyes are haunted by what he's seen and brim with tears, like a soldier returning from the battlefield. "I couldn't find her. I tried... I..."

"Trying isn't good enough." My spit sprays over his face. The Dukes should protect people. That's our purpose. How can we claim to protect strangers when we can't even protect the woman we love? "You said she'd be safe with you. You promised you'd never let her out of your fucking sight!"

Seb chokes and gasps for air. I want him to suffer. I want him to feel how I do, as if a pack of starving animals are feasting on my heart and picking it apart piece by piece. Callen hauls me back, wrapping his arms around my chest to restrain me.

"You don't want to do this, boss," Callen says. How the fuck does he know what I want? "As much as I want to see pretty boy's face re-arranged, this isn't the right time."

Seb clutches his neck, now marked from my hands.

"Fine," I relent, trying to shrug Callen off. He's never stepped into the role of a mediator before; that's something Bram used to do. "Let me go."

He reluctantly releases his hold, and I readjust my shirt to ensure it's not wrinkled while Seb doubles over and splutters.

I turn my back on them both, storm into the kitchen and search under the sink for the bottle of whiskey I spotted this morning. I grab it and take a swig. It does nothing to calm me, but the liquid torching my throat provides a distraction. Fire meets fire.

Seb limps into the room after me, followed by Callen, who creates a human barrier between us.

I take a steady breath to compose myself and order, "Tell me everything."

"There was an explosion," Seb says. "Half the manor has fallen down!"

"I don't care what happened to the manor," I snap. I couldn't give a shit whether they transported it into fucking space or an alien spaceship landed on its roof. "What happened to Rose?"

"She was with me one minute, then she went to the bathroom, then it happened, and she was gone."

"Nobody disappears in a puff of smoke."

"I tried to look for her," Seb answers earnestly. His voice is filled with a desperate yearning and a consuming drive to find her that I recognise, but I'm too busy processing my own emotions to manage his, too. "I tried to go back inside to look for her, but... the police... I couldn't... they wouldn't let me pass. I couldn't see her."

My head reels, simultaneously running through every possibility. We were just reunited, but is she really dead this time?

"I didn't see her body," Seb continues. "It's possible she was still somewhere inside the building, or she found another escape. People started to leave after it happened. Someone could have given her a lift out of there."

"I doubt the Collingsbrook's guests would have prioritised a stranger," Callen adds bitterly. He's right. If they were on the Titanic, Rose and the staff would have been last to be offered a lifeboat. They look after their own.

"You need to make calls," I order. There's no evidence to suggest anything's happened to Rose yet. We need all the facts. "Call anyone and everyone at the party to find out what happened. What caused the fire?" I press. "An explosion in the kitchen? Electrical problems? A fire-eater performance gone wrong?" Those parties often include circus acts to entertain the crowd. "What do you think caused it?"

He shifts his weight uncomfortably from one foot to the other.

"What is it?"

There's something he isn't telling me.

"When I was at the station, I had some time to think and go over everything. I saw something that looked unusual." Seb's Adam's apple bobs as he swallows hard. "I..."

"Spit it out, Seb," I growl, losing patience for his stuttering bullshit.

"I saw—"

My ringing phone cuts him off before he can respond. I jump to answer, hoping it's Rose, then realise there's no way it can be because she doesn't have a phone or means of contacting us. Why the hell didn't we buy her a replacement after Callen threw hers away? I was so fixated on sealing her away from the outside world for her safety that I didn't consider how we were isolating her from us, too.

"It's Spencer." I almost don't answer until I remember he was at the ball. He might have more information than Seb, who got whisked away in a police car. I answer and put him on speaker.

Spencer launches into a tirade without a greeting.

"You were supposed to protect me!" he rages. "The Collingsbrook Ball was a disaster!"

While he talks, Seb paces anxiously, mumbling like a madman. Callen fills the kettle and sets it to boil, then tears open a packet of Jammie Dodgers, completely unshaken.

"You sound like you're still alive to me," I bite back when Spencer finally stops for air. "What's the problem?"

"No thanks to the Dukes," he retorts. "The man who was supposed to protect me abandoned me at the first sign of trouble to chase after a whore!" Seb opens his mouth to argue, and I hold up one finger to silence him. We need to let Spencer have his temper tantrum. Like most children, he'll run out of steam eventually. "He left me!"

"I have a question for you, Spencer," I say, ignoring his ravings. "I want to ask you if you recognise a woman."

Callen freezes as he raises a biscuit to his mouth with

his tongue hanging out. He's eaten the top layer of the biscuit and is about to lick the raspberry jam layer.

"What're you talking about?" Spencer asks. "I was almost burned alive tonight, and now you want me to do an identification?"

"Exactly," I reply. "I'll send you a picture now." I select the image of him and Rose I found while searching his desk. "Now I want you to look and tell me who that woman is and everything you know about her."

# CHAPTER 8

## CALLEN

Seb's jaw drops as he peers over Freddie's shoulder to look at the photograph. This must be what he found from rummaging around Spencer's mansion and mentioned over the phone.

Well, shit. There's no doubt it's Rose, smiling at the camera next to that smarmy arse hole like butter wouldn't melt. If she's used to that standard of man, it's no surprise she gushed over my cock. I doubt Spencer Bexley knows where the clitoris is and likely thinks it's the name for a fancy seafood dish.

Freddie glares at Seb to stop him from asking more questions, but my thoughts jump ten steps ahead. Of course, I'm interested in what bullshit Spencer will say, but everything is beginning to make sense.

Rose is part of the Killers Club. I thought she was just another of their assassins. Someone paid for a hit, and she did the job, but seeing her with Spencer changes that. It's too much of a coincidence that she has a connection with him and for his men to be picked off one by one. She must be involved.

Killing Lord McGowan gave me justice. Is Rose seeking retribution of her own? It's hard to know how much of the story she told us was true, based on her being a compulsive liar living a double life. But we know she had a sister who died five years ago. Whoever killed Spencer's men held a serious grudge. His men must have done something terrible enough to warrant their gruesome end. Something like killing her sister.

Spencer pauses on the other end of the line as he reviews the photograph.

"I don't understand…" His voice trails off. I don't need to see his face to know that motherfucker is guilty. "Where did you get that?"

"Touchy," I mutter.

"Where I got it from doesn't matter," Freddie counters. He's regained control of himself after unleashing the beast lurking behind his measured exterior. He's like Jekyll and Hyde, moving between different personas. "Who is she?"

"I can't remember her name," Spencer dismisses. He's being too casual, casual enough to cement my suspicion that he's trying hard to conceal something. "It might have been Lily… Violet… something like that. We went on a few dates. Nothing serious. You know what it's like."

Freddie's forehead crinkles as his eyebrows lower. A wild storm eclipses his features, taking over his face. "Do you keep pictures of all the women you date?"

"What is this? An interrogation?" Spencer snaps. "I've already told you. I don't really remember her. Although now that you mention it, something is coming back to me." He pauses. "I think she died a few years ago. There was an accident. Why are you interested, anyway? Were you looking for her number?"

I clench my teeth as the kettle bubbles behind me.

"I have my reasons," Freddie replies.

"Why do I feel like I'm on trial?" There's a bang in the background as Spencer slams his fist on a table. "Need I remind you that I'm your client? I've paid good money for your protection, and I don't think I'm getting the best service. I had high hopes for the Dukes, but the rumours are wrong. You're a bunch of amateurs."

Seb cracks his knuckles. "I'll show you amateurs."

"Our contract is terminated," Spencer says. "I'm going to find a real security firm that knows what they're doing. A security firm that will find answers and make sure a bomb doesn't get smuggled into a ball."

"A bomb?"

"That's what they're saying," Spencer says, "not that I'd expect you and your team to know that, considering your—"

Freddie hangs up to end Spencer's incessant whine and turns to Seb. "You said you saw something unusual tonight. What was it?"

"Lord McGowan's arms were blasted off." Seb grimaces. "I thought it might have been part of a gas explosion, but after hearing from Spencer, I'd say a bomb is pretty likely."

*Shit!* Why did Seb have to mention his name?

"Lord McGowan?" Freddie pushes for confirmation. "Are you sure?"

"Positive," Seb confirms.

Freddie whirls around to face me. A foreboding silence stretches out as he sets me in his murderous sights. He knows my history and what Lord McGowan did to Tilly. I expected him to find out eventually, but I didn't expect it to come out so soon.

Seb looks between the two of us. "What's going—"

"Quiet!" Freddie roars. He picks up my mug and hurls it at the wall. There goes a perfectly good Tetley tea bag—if it was a Yorkshire Tea, I'd hope he'd have shown more respect. Freddie advances, squaring up to me shoulder-to-shoulder. "What did you do, Callen?"

"Look, I had an opportunity." I back away slowly and hold up my hands. "Don't tell me you wouldn't have done the same."

I stumble on a broken ceramic shard. Stupid mug.

"The Dukes protect people." Freddie follows me. "We don't kill for revenge. We're not the Killers Club. That's not who we are."

"But this is different," I insist. "You know what he did. I had a chance, and I took it. If I came to you, you'd have stopped me."

"And for good reason! How many more people did you kill tonight because they got caught in the crossfire?" he asks, shaking in anger. "Time and time again, I've given you chances. So many fucking chances. I asked you to join the Dukes to offer you a lifeline. I gave you the opportunity to prove yourself and show that you're one of us, and this is how you repay me?"

"Wait, you did it?" Seb frowns in confusion. No shit, Sherlock. Keep up! "But how did you get past security?"

I shrug. "I might have had some help."

"You got her to do it." Freddie's nostrils flare. "How? Did you blackmail her? What did you threaten her with?"

I laugh coldly. "Your little angel didn't require much persuading after I gave her the best orgasm of her life."

Seb's cheeks flush in jealous anger. If they're going to kill me, they may as well know the truth about their precious fucking princess.

"You're lying." Freddie refuses to believe it. "She'd never be interested in you."

"Why don't you ask Seb?" I grin. "He'll tell you that's not true."

Seb's mouth opens and then closes again like a gasping goldfish. "I... I..."

"You never told Freddie about what happened between us that night, did you?" I goad him. "How you walked in on me fucking her. How you saw how badly she wanted to fuck me, so you joined in."

Seb's guilty expression confirms what I'm saying is true.

"What did you do to her?" Freddie demands. "Where is she now?"

"Beats me," I reply. "She did what I asked, then left. She's smart—smarter than you two give her credit for."

"You could have killed her!" Seb dives at me, but Freddie hauls him back. "You're a monster!"

They think they're superior, but the difference between me and them is that I'm not afraid to face the truth.

I'm not like Seb. He became a Duke to break out of his family's mould and do something meaningful, but he doesn't admit that he gets his kicks from the violent parts of our jobs. He likes making them pay.

I'm not the same as Freddie. He presents himself as gallant and wanting to right past wrongs, but he's blind to how we're no better. He needs to embrace his true nature. Only he can't because of his skewed perception that it'd justify what happened to his family.

Bram, if he's still alive, is just as damaged and broken. He thinks being a Duke will put his skills to good use, but he never saw that he was swapping one set of rules for another.

I am done pretending and complying with Freddie's bullshit rules. I'm unapologetically me, and until they can face who they are, I'll never belong here.

"You think the Dukes are protectors, but we're not," I say. "We're killers, and I'm the only one with the fucking balls to say it. Rose is gone, and who can blame her? You thought bringing her to a safe house and playing happy family was what she wanted, but you were wrong. She saw us for who we are, and she fucking ran."

"She ran because of you!" Freddie explodes. He's delusional. "You made her detonate a fucking bomb and left her alone! That's why she's gone!"

"Here we go again with the poor Rose sob story." I put on a childish voice and stick out my bottom lip. "Boo-fucking-hoo, Rose is the victim! Rose is a princess who we need to sweep in and save!" My jaw sets, and my eyes narrow into slits. "You don't know a thing about her. You're both living in a fantasy world. Until you snap out of it, you'll see nothing clearly. You're mad at me, but this is your fault. You're the ones who brought a stranger into our lives. What did you think would happen? Did you think we'd all skip off into the sunset to live happily ever after? This is real fucking life, and that's never going to happen."

"You've broken our rules for the last time," Freddie growls. His muscles flex through his shirt. "Leave, or I'll rip your throat out."

"There." I point at him. "That's the man who I came to work for!" I shake my head. "Not the pussy who can't face his true self."

I thought that working with them would help me. I even had some bullshit idea that it might turn me into a better person and give me a new family to look after, but it's only shown that I don't belong.

"We don't need you," Freddie says. "I'm done with cleaning up your messes. You're a curse, Callen."

It's true. Trouble and death follow me. I was a curse to my daughter. I'm better off on my own. A lone wolf. That's how it's meant to be.

I storm out of the cottage and slam the door behind me, making the wall rattle. I'll leave them to rot in their self-created misery, but that doesn't mean I'm done with Rose…

Now that I'm not a Duke, I'll have a lot of free time on my hands, and I've always enjoyed playing cat and mouse.

# CHAPTER 9



t's only been three days since I returned to HQ, and I'm going stir-crazy. *Thwack*! I drive my fist into the punching bag. Even pretending to dislocate Spencer's jaw isn't helping, and thinking of ways to hurt him is usually my number one mood booster.

Alaric hasn't allowed me to venture outside for fear the Dukes are hiding around corners. Although he hasn't said it, I think the real reason for keeping me locked away is to make sure I won't run back to them. Even if I wanted to see them again, which would be a terrible idea, I have no idea where to find them.

Like when I first joined the club, Alaric is trying to instil a routine in me again. I used to welcome the structure, but the restriction is suffocating now. It reminds me of how I felt as a teenager when our parents permanently locked our windows to stop Daisy and me from sneaking out to beach parties. Daisy broke her arm at one of the parties, so I could understand their reasoning, but still...

"Hey!" Stephanie pokes her head around the door of

the training area and waves a Starbucks iced latte in my direction. "Want one?"

"I'd love one," I groan gratefully. I take off my gloves and stroll over to accept my drink. "But I'd love to breathe fresh air more. How much longer are you going to keep me here? I already look like Casper the Ghost. I need some sun!"

"It's better for you to be here right now," she replies. "I'm sure Sebastian Montgomery gave you enough vitamin D to keep you going for a while."

"But I want to do something!" I sound like a petulant child, but I don't care. I like to be busy. "I can make myself useful. With the Tweedles gone and Jonathon down, you must need help."

"We've got extra help," Stephanie says. "Just keep following orders, and you'll be back in the field in no time."

"Yeah," I grumble sarcastically, "if the Lotus doesn't steal all my work."

She changes the subject. "Have you been keeping up with news on the Collingsbrook Ball?"

"Duh," I reply. "What else have I got to do?"

It's also hard to miss when the story is all every TV channel and newspaper has been covering. Victim portraits are displayed alongside their names and lists of all their amazing work for charities. When they're not showing glowing profiles, there are reams of interviews with snivelling mourners whose eyes sparkle with the greed of someone who will soon be inheriting a holiday home in the Bahamas.

"Our sources on the inside say it was a bomb," she says. "Despite what the press is reporting."

"Really? No shit," I say, keeping my tone measured. "Is Penelope looking into it?"

The stories talk about how it was a freak accident caused by faulty wiring. The establishment wants to keep the truth hidden, especially because the royal family was in attendance—one Guy Fawkes day a year is enough.

"Between other jobs." Stephanie shrugs. "Besides, we've got other jobs that don't involve solving mysteries. Have you seen what they're saying about your prince charming?"

The paparazzi have loved blasting photographs of Sebastian Montgomery, the disgraced royal who spent some time behind bars, everywhere. It provides light relief and redirection to distraction from the tragedy.

"Who cares?" I deflect. "Do you have any jobs for me?"

"Actually, yes." She swirls her straw around her green juice. She's on a diet right now where she only eats green foods. If she's not careful, she'll turn into an ogre. "Alaric wants you to get more information out of Bram."

"Bram? Remind me why we're keeping him alive again?" Freddie and Seb care about him, but all I can think of whenever I hear his name is how he used to work for Spencer and that he was there the night Daisy died. "Isn't there someone else who can babysit?"

"We're low on numbers, as you've already pointed out."

"What about the Lotus?" I ask. "Or is she too good for that?"

"All our other agents are busy," she shuts me down. So I'm getting the grunt work as punishment. Figures. "We want you to start today."

One job hasn't gone my way, and I'm back in training

again. I need to get information out of Bram to regain Alaric's trust.

"Fine, but I'll get to him when I'm done here," I mumble. "It's not like he's going anywhere."

I trail back to my room, my bad mood causing me to drag my feet. Once inside, I peel off my sweaty clothes and head for the shower in my ensuite. I stand under the spray as it warms, taking deep breaths to relieve some of the frustration. It doesn't work.

I shut my eyes. The warm water flows over my skin, and I feel their hands on me. Fuck! How is this possible? I keep my eyes shut. I allow myself a moment to remember just how fucking good their touch felt, and how Freddie looked at me like I was the only person in the world.

My hands slide down, over my stomach and between my legs. I part my thighs wider, moving under the spray to allow the water to hit my clit. I touch myself, moaning into the steam, thinking about Seb's wet tongue exploring me. I slide a finger along my entrance, remembering the weight of Freddie on top of me, and… *STOP!*

*You have to stop.*

I open my eyes, and I'm back in the present. I twist the temperature dial to freezing, hoping to halt my desire. A forbidden desire I shouldn't have. But the coldness doesn't help. It reminds me of Callen. How he sprawled me over his bike. How the breeze chilled my arse as he railed into me, taking and punishing me with his cock.

*Why can't I get them out of my head?*

Maybe Alaric's right to be worried about my motives when I don't understand them myself…

Alaric wants to wait for them to come to us, and when they do, I'll have to confront them head-on and do what I avoided when I was with them: I'll have to kill them.

# CHAPTER 10

## CALLEN

I sit in the corner of the gentlemen's club, slumped in a chair with crispy upholstery. Through the dimly lit room, I catch the eye of the beauty who slides her legs up and down the greasy pole. She swings her bouncy brown hair over her shoulder, and a mischievous smile flicks over her pout as her gaze meets mine, making her intentions clear.

The pink strobe light hits her face, accentuating her filler-pumped lips. She runs her pointed tongue over them as she vigorously humps the pole with her groin. If she can pound against metal like that, she'll take my cock with no problem.

I lean back and sip my drink, watching her perform the rest of the song. Other girls dance on different podiums, but they don't keep my attention. They're all too busy fluttering their false eyelashes at other schmucks. That, and the fact they look vaguely familiar. I'm a regular and have slept with most of these girls, but the brunette is new. Fresh blood.

After the song finishes, I return to my beer, letting her come to me.

She slinks over to my table, swaying her hips. "Do you want a private dance, Mister?" she asks in a thick cockney accent.

I shake my wallet. "Show me the way."

Her entire face lights up. My monster will make a change from the flaccid pickles she spends most of her time grinding against. She takes my hand to lead me through the club.

It's busy tonight. More tits shake than I have time to check out. A busty girl in black pasties grabs my attention. Her soft curves remind me of… nope, I'm not going there. *Fuck that bitch.* I down my glass to push thoughts of Rose away and wipe my foamy moustache with my sleeve.

"What's your name?" I ask the hooker, not that I care. Every hole is a goal.

"Missy," she replies as we approach a bouncer who guards a private corridor. He looks out for the girls and nods to let us through.

Doors leading to small private cubicles are lined up on both walls. It's a seedy place with purple velvet wallpaper that'd glow under ultraviolet light—some of it is probably mine. This club doesn't have a look-but-no-touch rule which is why it's one of my favourites.

"This way." She tugs me eagerly to the last vacant room, almost yanking my arm out of its socket. Someone's thirsty.

Once inside, I make myself comfortable on the pink velour bench while Missy draws the thick curtains over the viewing window in the door. They host peep shows sometimes too.

To our left, rhythmic noises that sound like a seal clapping signifies a cunt that's had to use an entire bottle of lube to get the job done.

"Someone's having a good time," I comment.

Tinny music blasts through a small speaker in the corner of the cubicle. Missy clambers onto my lap and starts gyrating her hips. I tuck a twenty-pound note into her bra.

"Do you like that?" she purrs, pushing her fake tits into my face.

Her perfume is overpoweringly sweet, making me want to gag. Usually, my cock would be throbbing and ready for action, but… nothing.

She grabs my head and shoves me into her cleavage. Up close, I have a better view of her streaky fake tan. When she pulls back, giving me a chance to breathe, I notice she has two-inch thick make-up plastered over her face and wonky lip liner. She'd look good enough for a one-time shag after a night out, but you'd be running from her in the morning.

She flips around. Okay, this will do it—at least I won't have to see her face. She shakes her round arse, twerking on me, then grabs my hands and makes me run them over her hips.

"Is everything okay?" she asks nervously.

My cock hasn't even twitched. It's shrivelled up like a deflated balloon exposed to negative temperatures.

"Everything's fine," I growl. "I'm paying you to dance, so fucking dance."

She climbs off and drops to her knees. Her talons are three inches long; she slides them up my legs and digs into my thighs. I usually have no issue with my hardware, but my cock stays lifeless.

"Do you want me to do something else?" she asks,

eyeing my crotch. What's happening? I can fuck anyone anytime! "What do you like?"

What I like are redheaded serial killers with snarky mouths.

Thinking of Rose makes my dick stir instantly. I picture spanking her round arse bent over my bike and seeing my pink handprint against the paleness of her skin.

I clear my throat and stand up. "I think I'm done here."

"But I can do whatever you like," she whines, reeking of desperation. She could stuff my cock and balls into her arsehole, but it wouldn't change anything. She can't shapeshift into someone else. She isn't Rose. "I'm down for anything. All you have to do is tell me what you want."

"I want you to get out of my way," I snarl.

She jumps back as I tear open the curtain and march away.

"He didn't pay!" Missy shrieks like a banshee, almost shattering my eardrums.

I spin. "I'm not paying for something I don't see any value in." My lip curls, looking her up and down. "You're lucky to have got twenty quid."

The security guard, lying in wait like a hungry dragon protecting its treasure, launches into action. He doesn't scare me. If he thinks he'll beat me into paying this whore any more money, he's mistaken.

I ready myself for a fight and throw myself in first. The guard swings, but he's not skilled or trained, relying purely on his size to propel him forward. I dodge his advances and retaliate, punching him hard in the jaw. He drops like a sack of spuds, and I jump on top of him.

*Crack!*

His nose breaks under my fist.

*Smash!*

I dislodge a few teeth. He splutters and coughs them up, spraying me with blood.

"Stop!" Missy yells. She climbs onto my back, trying to pull me off him and clinging on like I'm a Bucking Bronco.

The doors to the other booths fly open. There's a flurry of zipping trousers as other dancers rush to protect him. The gaggle of bitches scratch and claw at my cheeks and shoulders, but it doesn't bother me.

The guard loses consciousness.

"You're going to kill him!" Missy wails, but I'm too far gone. I've seen red. "We've called the police!"

A run-in with the coppers would scupper my plans. I stop, throwing Missy off my back, and rise to my feet. The other girls press their backs against the wall in fear. None of them dare to say any more.

I spit at my feet.

"I won't be back," I hiss.

What the hell has Rose turned me into?

# CHAPTER 11
## SEB

Freddie's bloodshot eyes don't stray from his laptop screen when I pick up the cold, untouched mug of coffee next to him. I sniff the liquid suspiciously. It's instant. Fuck, this is bad. I don't think I've ever seen him drink an instant coffee since we've known each other, aside from the time I pranked him on April Fools'.

"Do you want another?" I ask.

He ignores me, madly tapping away on his laptop and monitoring the news for any updates. He's called in favours with some of his old friends from the force. A source confirmed a bomb obliterated Collingsbrook Manor, but they're keeping the truth out of the public eye. Their investigation is at the highest security clearance level. From what we've heard, the police are chasing their tails and are no closer to finding the person responsible.

"Hello!" I wave a hand in front of his vacant face. "Earth to Freddie!"

"Can't you see I'm busy?" he snaps, then sighs, pinching the bridge of his nose in frustration. "I can't find anything."

We've increased our efforts in our search for the Killers Club and rescuing Bram if he's still alive. We're looking through files of mysterious deaths and seeing if we can make any links. The safe house living room has been transformed into our crime investigation room, pinning papers and photographs to boards on the walls and using string to connect the dots. Then there's Rose…

She vanished into thin air.

We received confirmation that her body wasn't among the dead at the manor. The police are speaking to everyone present that night, but they haven't been able to track her down either. Freddie's contact will notify us if they hear anything, but she's been in witness protection before. She's used to disappearing and mustn't want to be found, although I can't shake the disappointment that she's not been in touch. It's Callen's fault; he scared her away.

"There's nothing on CCTV," Freddie says. He's spent painstaking hours trawling through footage from a camera close to Rose's flat. He hasn't been eating or sleeping properly, and finding Rose has become an obsession. "If she's not gone home, where did she go?"

"She's not dead," I remind him.

"Not dead isn't good enough." He inflates his cheeks with air, then releases it in an exasperated puff. "We're missing something."

Being here, secluded, isn't good for him. He's going to lose his mind if we stay cooped up in the cottage for much longer, but we can't risk returning to the Dukes' central base after the Killers Club compromised it. Thankfully, it's not our only property in the city. Returning to London soon could break Freddie's computer trance.

"We'll find them," I reassure him. "Both of them."

"You don't know that," he growls.

I don't, but I feel it. We're down to two Dukes. While Freddie is on a downward spiral, I need to step up as his second in command. We need to fix this. Our family is falling apart, and we're destroying ourselves without any help from the Killers Club.

The breeze whistles through the floorboards upstairs. I'm not used to a house being so quiet. Callen's been gone a few days, and his presence has left a gaping hole behind. When Freddie told me about his daughter and what Lord McGowan did, I could understand Callen's motivations, but putting Rose in harm's way was unforgivable.

I groan as my phone rings. Mum has already called five times today, but I keep sending her to voicemail. It's easier than listening to another lecture about how much of a disappointment I am to the family.

While I reject the call, a knock at the front door startles us. *Is it her?* Freddie leaps up, vaulting over the chair and racing to it. My heartbeat increases, daring to hope, until I hear my brother's voice.

"Where is he?" Ralph demands in his usual entitled fashion.

Freddie mutters something and steps aside for Ralph to stroll in.

"So this is where you've been hiding out," Ralph says, surveying the clues we've stuck to the walls. "Bloody hell, I thought you were losing the plot at the ball, but this is… something else. Don't you think this has gone on for long enough?"

Freddie barges past, knocking into Ralph's shoulder, grabbing his laptop, and stomping up the stairs. He doesn't get involved in my family business, but, for once, it'd be nice to have his support.

"This isn't supposed to be a place for waifs and strays,"

Ralph comments as he leaves. Although, he doesn't give Freddie the same look of disgust that he gave Callen. "This is an official building."

"A building no one has used for years," I retort. "How did you know where to find me?"

Ralph ignores me and continues, "We knew you weren't in London, and Mother found out we were being billed for energy usage here. Do you realise how embarrassing that was for her? Even our uncle heard about it!"

So? The King has enough money. An electricity bill wasn't going to threaten the Crown jewels.

"Don't you have your own family to look after, or is life not so perfect, after all?" I ask. "Chasing around after your screw-up of a younger brother seems to be a regular theme lately."

He scowls. "There are things I'd rather be doing than cleaning up your mess."

"Why don't you mind your own damn business?" I cross my arms. Ralph's gaze strays to an overspilling stack of dirty dishes piled in the kitchen sink in the next room. "I'd offer you tea, but I don't think you'll be staying long."

"You're coming with me," Ralph says. "Back to London."

"Says who? You can't make me do anything," I scoff. "Unlike you, I don't rely on our family's money for a living."

"This isn't about money," Ralph snaps. We look similar. We have the same white-blonde hair, but Ralph is more polished and rounder. He reminds me of an overgrown cherub who acts like a cunt. "This is about making things right for the family."

"Does it hurt?" I ask him. "Having your nose buried up the Crown's arse all the fucking time?"

"You hate being royal, but do you think companies would have let you invest in them if it wasn't for the Montgomery name?" Ralph snickers. "You've made your wealth, but don't pretend you haven't used our family connections to get it." His words leave a bitter taste in my mouth. He's right, but it doesn't take away how hard I've worked to be successful. "Your reputation is in tatters, and Mother plans to fix it."

"A plan?" I snort. Mum loves scheming. At the last royal wedding, she devised a scheme to maximise our press exposure. This will be another opportunity to seize the spotlight. "I don't care what people think of me."

"You don't, but this isn't about you." Ralph's voice turns stern and gruff like Dad's. We don't see our father often. He's a man of few words, but his strict orders and commitment to tradition terrified me as a child. "You have to do this."

Freddie appears in the doorway and leans against the frame. He must have been listening in the entire time. "Ralph's right."

"Thank you." Ralph grins in triumph, delighted to have an ally. "Whoever you are."

"You can't mean that." I look pleadingly at Freddie. "There's... a lot to do."

"You need to make it right with your family," Freddie says. His eyes glance in my direction, but he's looking straight through me. His mind is elsewhere. "You don't get a second chance with them."

"Pack your things." Ralph claps his hands. "Chop, chop!"

I glower at him. "I'll pack in my own time."

"And you should clear out this place." His nose wrinkles. "It's a mess, and Mother is going to cut the power any minute now."

"Great," I grumble. "So, what is her grand plan?"

"She has something in mind to correct your public image." Whatever it is, it can't be good…

# CHAPTER 12

## CALLEN

Nothing ruins the freeing feeling of the wind rushing through your hair more than a flashing warning light.

*Shit.*

Thankfully, there's a petrol station ahead. I swerve to stop, fill the tank, and head inside the shop to pay.

I saunter through the aisles. It's been a few days since I've eaten a good meal. I grab a share bag of cheese and onion crisps, then pass the minimal selection of fruit. Gotta get my vitamins. I grab an apple and head to the checkout, tossing it like a tennis ball.

"Pump nine," I say, putting the items on the counter. "And these."

A pock-marked teenager whose greasy hair hangs around his chin like wet curtains presses a few buttons. "That'll be twenty-two pounds and twelve pence."

Daylight fucking robbery. I grunt as I dig my hands into my pockets. There are two crinkled ten-pound notes, and the rest is in coppers. I carefully count them, sliding the coins across to him in neatly stacked piles.

"You're ten pence short," the kid observes.

"Well done, wee lad," I say. "You can do maths." I reach into my other pocket to find more. There's nothing. "Why don't we call it even?"

The kid clears his throat, deciding now's the right time to squeeze out a pubic hair. "I'm afraid I can't do that."

"Can't do that?" I mimic.

Do I look like a man open to being challenged by a teenager who needs a wash?

"N-n-n-no," he stammers. His confidence wilts like his newly found testosterone. "You'll have to p-p-put something back."

"Will I?" I take a bite out of the crunchy apple and chew it for a few seconds. Once it's turned into gooey mush, I spit it out on top of the change. "There you go."

The kid's mouth falls open as I grab the crisps and head out of the shop, sticking my middle finger up behind me. Little shit. Let that be a life lesson. I stash my goods underneath the bike seat, climb on, then start the engine and speed away.

I've spent the last week searching for answers. Answers that Freddie and Seb will be looking for too. But they're missing the biggest piece of the puzzle: who Rose really is.

First, I found out everything I could about Matteo Santiago, the man she claimed killed her sister, and how he died. Rose's story doesn't add up. I know people in bad circles who told me about Matteo's past. He was an abusive trafficker with a violent appetite and enjoyed killing women in a particular way. Car crashes wouldn't do it for him. Instead, I believe the Killers Club—maybe even Rose herself—was responsible for his death. Rose is smart enough to know that lying is easier if you stay close to the truth.

If my theory is correct, it helps support my initial suspicions. Spencer could be responsible for Rose's sister's death, and she's killing his men for revenge. Lucky for me, I've contacted someone who can help prove it…

"Come on," I growl, revving the engine to the max and willing the bike to go quicker.

I swing into the car park beside a remote greasy spoon off the motorway. Through the cafe window, I see he's already here. It's been a year since we saw each other and the first time we've spoken since I joined the Dukes.

A bell above the door jingles as I enter. My thick leathers stick to me as a wall of heat, and the smell of cheap grilled meat hits me. I trudge towards the table where he's sitting.

He sips his coffee, a thick tar-like substance that's as black as his heart. I cast him in my dark shadow, and he gestures at the seat opposite him. "I was beginning to think you weren't coming."

Torean's face lights up in a twisted grin as I sit down. Looking at him is unnerving, like staring at myself in a mirror.

"It's been a long time," Torean says. "I'm starting to think you only get in touch when you want something."

I narrow my eyes. "Can you give me the information I asked for or not?"

My twin's laughter rings around the diner. We're identical, aside from his lack of ink and shorter hair. He wears a black shirt with the top buttons loose which, for him, is a casual look. If people think I'm bad, they should meet him.

When I left for medical school to escape our Glasgow council estate shithole, Torean stayed and worked the streets. He built a drug empire and moved to Edinburgh. During my medical career, we rarely talked. He met Tilly once, a few months before she died, but it was easier to pretend my twin worked overseas than admit the truth— even my ex-wife didn't know what he did for a living. I couldn't risk anything muddying my stellar reputation.

"You asked me the same question a year ago when Frederick James came sniffing around for information." Torean's eyes twinkle with malice. "The answer is the same. I don't keep records of favours I do for friends. Why do you think I'd tell you anything now, *Vincent*?"

I grit my teeth at his use of my pseudonym.

"Because I know that you were hiding something." I didn't push Torean for answers last time because it scared me to know what they were and how the truth could compromise my spot in the Dukes. "And because this time, it's not Freddie wanting the answer. I'm asking for me."

"You should be able to remember yourself." Torean takes a photograph out of his pocket and turns it to show me. The grainy image shows Freddie and Rose standing on the pavement of a London street while a black cab drives past. My stomach twists as he points at the cab. "You were the one driving and surveilling her that night."

"Do you think I'd be here if I remembered?" I snap.

After Tilly died, I grew out my hair. With the money I had left from the divorce, I bought my bike and spent months travelling around Scotland, taking out my anger on anyone who got in my way.

There were bar fights, brawls at football games, and bare-knuckle boxing matches. I developed a taste for violence and became unrecognisable from the man I used to be. When I crossed paths with my brother again by chance, he watched as I almost killed a man in a street fight. He was proud I was finally fulfilling my family's destiny. The Campbell clan has a bloody history, and he wanted me to work for him... so I did.

"Why do you care about this, anyway?" Torean stashes the photograph away. "I'll tell you what I told Freddie: I asked you to watch the bar and call a number when the ginger bitch left. How do you expect me to remember who the job was for? I don't keep any records."

When Freddie found me a year ago, he'd been tracking my alter ego—Vincent Pew—for months. He was investigating Rose's four-year-old disappearance and found footage of a black cab registered under my alias near the scene. When Rose vanished, I was high on a concoction of drugs. I told him I did some surveillance work for my brother, but the details were hazy. Freddie was pissed I couldn't give him more details, so he spoke to Torean but got no leads.

As Freddie and I talked more, we found we had a lot in common. He saw potential in my skills and showed me I could be more than my brother's bitch. He gave me hope that I'd make a difference by joining the Dukes. Yeah, fucking right...

"You're lying." I cross my arms. "I didn't push last time, but I know you remember every job you do."

Torean smirks. My brother's a criminal, but he's one of the most intelligent people I know. He has an almost photographic memory.

"Hypothetically, if I could tell you who asked me to watch the girl," Torean says, drumming his fingers on the table. "I'd need something from you in return."

"Cut the bullshit. What do you want?"

He chuckles and reaches into his trouser pocket for a

brown envelope and pushes it across the table. I tear open the seal and shake out a fake passport and driving licence. I open it to see my face staring back at me with 'Vincent Pew' written next to it. He wants me to become him again. A part of myself I made Freddie swear to keep secret. A part of myself with no boundaries at all.

"One kill, that's all," Torean says. "I give you a name, and you take care of it, then I'll tell you who wanted to know where the pocket-rocket was that night."

I don't need time to think about it.

"Done."

# CHAPTER 13

## BRAM

Alaric gave me a job to do, but how can I test Ivy's loyalty if she doesn't come to the dungeon?

While I've been waiting for her to show over the last few days, he's given me a few privileges: better food, regular hose-downs, and clean clothes. It's not a luxury spa stay, but it's an improvement.

Is this how the Killers Club usually secures their agents? Do they kidnap and break people down until they can't take anymore, only to give them a lifeline they have no choice but to accept?

101… 102… 103…

I recount the points on the floor tiles, running my fingers over the cracks. When I've finished that, I'll count the number of bricks, then start over again. It helps pass the time and keeps my mind occupied. Time blurs together. I've lost track of the days passing, and it's impossible to tell whether it's day or night.

Sometimes I hear voices. They talk in my head. I have conversations with myself and think about how things could have been. The lack of sleep doesn't help. Whenever I drift off,

I'm woken by their screams. Screams of women and children. Then, when I wake, I remember this is exactly what I deserve.

Stephanie and Alaric come and go. Sometimes together. Sometimes apart. I listen to snatches of their conversations. They're both here now. They left a ketchup and butter sandwich for me and are heading back into the depths of the building.

"Fishy wants to hire for another job," Stephanie says. She talks quietly enough that most people would struggle to hear her, but my senses are amplified. I know every sound in this place. I distinguish the noise of the dripping leaky pipe, the boiler's whir, and the opening and closing of the doors trapping me here. "What do we tell him?"

They never address their clients by their names around me and only use code words, but I recognise that nick-name. It's distinct. Unless it's a strange coincidence, I think they're referring to Christopher Trout—one of Spencer's right-hand men. A man who was there the night Spencer forced Ivy and Daisy's car off the road.

"I'll sort it myself as soon as we receive payment," Alaric says venomously. "Have him send it to the usual account." He stops walking. "Don't give me that look, Steph. Quit worrying about—"

"I just think you need to be careful, that's all," she interrupts. "We have to handle this delicately."

"Like how you deployed the Lotus to kill Doyle?" he sneers sarcastically. "Yeah, real fucking delicate. Don't lecture me about how to do my job. You need to remember your place here. You're not the boss; I am. Maybe it's time you remember that."

She yelps like a wounded dog. I hear his shoes hitting the concrete as he storms away and slams the dungeon door closed with a crash. I can't hear her footsteps. She stays put. She sniffles and takes a few deep breaths before following him and clicking the door closed softly behind her. It's the first time I've heard them argue.

A few hours pass, and I return to the monotony of counting to keep my memories away.

56… 57… 58…

Suddenly, the dungeon door hits the wall, and I jump to my feet. It's too soon for them to be bringing my next meal, which means…

"Ohhhh, Bram!" Her sing-song, playful voice makes the raised, angry mark on the centre of my chest sting. I've become accustomed to the constant pain, and it doesn't burn as much as it used to. "Are you awake? It's time to play." She makes her way to my cell and opens the hatch. Her brown eyes peer through and her skin crinkles at their edges, from a smile I can't see. "Have you missed me? It's time we had a catch-up."

My expression remains deadpan. She doesn't know it, but she's the one undertaking a test… and she's my ticket out of here.

When I'm breathing fresh air again, I'll have more control over what happens next, and I can come up with a real plan.

"I've brought you a present." She lobs a notebook through the hatch, followed by an onslaught of biro bullets. I imagine her pouting as she mocks me in a high-pitched voice. "You're not being very grateful. I thought you'd be pleased to see me."

If she expects me to be thankful, she can choke on my fucking dick. She snaps the hatch shut, and I hear her back slide down on the other side of the door to sit on the floor.

I don't move. Not yet. I must plan my moves carefully, so she suspects nothing.

I need her to trust me enough to set me free. 4830. That's the code to my cell door. All she needs to do is put in those numbers. There'll be no violence involved. No blood. No killing. I'll approach testing her like a good old-fashioned puzzle. All I have to do is work out how Ivy Penrose's brain works and dissect it like a complex code until I get my answer. She's going to be my most challenging code to crack.

"Are you ready to answer my questions?" she asks.

Game fucking on.

# CHAPTER 14
## CALLEN

Blood flecks spray over my face like rain droplets. I grunt and plunge the knife into his chest for the third time. His rib cage cracks against the blade as I chip the bone. One wound to the neck did the trick and severed the artery, but a few more jabs for luck won't hurt. He died instantly, but using his body as a pincushion is a great way to relieve some stress. I imagine it's Freddie. The fucker shouldn't have spoken to me how he did.

"Jacob?" A woman's voice cuts over the noise of the cars racing down the nearby street, making me pause. "Jacob?"

Fuck, I have to hurry. I grab his ankles and drag the body deeper into the dark alleyway where my stolen getaway car's waiting. Jacob Bryan is heavier than he looks. I have to use all my strength to hoist him into the boot. I've spent the last few days watching him and seized the opportunity when he was walking back to his flat alone. He visited the Italian at the end of the road and was carrying home dinner with a bouquet, which I assume was for him and a date.

"You shouldn't have been a traitor," I hiss to the corpse as I slam the boot shut. "That's from Torean."

I don't know what Jacob did wrong, and I don't care. His death will give me the answers I need, plus a family-sized lasagne with garlic bread.

I get back into the car. My hands are soaked with his blood, so I grab a towel—I came prepared—to mop up the mess. I take off my T-shirt and bundle it into a black bag before putting on a fresh one. I need to look acceptable from the chest upwards, at least. *That'll do.*

I switch on the headlights and head off. Further down the street, I see the woman calling Jacob's name. Her short, blonde, curly hair bounces around her shoulders. She's wearing a pretty floral dress—too pretty for sitting around the house. She's made an effort for a special occasion. A birthday or anniversary, maybe? I'll have to stop by another time now that she's newly single.

I tap my fingers on the wheel while I wait at the junction. The woman's head swivels in my direction as I pull out and take a right turn.

She freezes on the pavement as our eyes meet. Her mouth falls open, and all the colour drains from her rosy cheeks. What's her problem? She looks like she's seen a ghost.

I push her shell-shocked face out of my mind and join the traffic, keeping strictly to the speed limit while Jacob rattles around in the boot like a ball bearing in a can of spray paint.

My work is done. I call Torean to let him know, and he answers on the first ring. "Well?"

"It's done," I say. "Now it's your turn to uphold our deal."

"I need proof."

Does my accent make me sound as annoying and smug as he does?

"Torean," I warn. "Don't push your fucking luck. I've done what you asked."

"Fine," he relents, yawning. I grind my teeth. "One of my men called in a favour for a friend to get a weapons discount. It was a rich prick… Blakely… Brexley… Bexley. That's it. Spencer Bexley."

I fucking knew it. How angry must Rose have been to discover the Dukes were protecting him? I'm surprised she didn't butcher us in our beds. If the roles were reversed, I would have.

I'm about to hang up when Torean adds, "Don't be a stranger again, Callen."

"Fuck you."

"Fuck you too."

That's the closest we'll ever get to saying we love each other in our own way. He cackles as I end the call.

Now all I have to do is get rid of the body and head back to the shitty hotel I booked for the night. I know the manager there. He doesn't ask questions and won't blink at my blood-soaked jeans.

I'm one step closer to finding my princess.

# CHAPTER 15
## SEB

We've moved into one of the many properties I own under different aliases. It's incredible what you can do in the name of discretion when you're a member of the royal family. The flat we're staying in is much smaller than our townhouse base, but we have a small weapons store and two bedrooms—enough space for what we need. It's on the twentieth floor and gives us an incredible view of the London Eye.

"I'm leaving," I call to Freddie.

He's sitting in front of a computer screen like a zombie with a half-empty bottle of vodka next to him. He's given up pouring it into a glass and slugs straight from the bottle. He's hit rock bottom, and nothing I seem to do makes any difference.

We've been back in London for three days, and the longer he searches, the more dead ends he finds.

"Freddie?" I say again to make sure he's heard me. "I'll be back later. Can I get you anything?"

He grunts in reply. I'll take that as a no. I check my reflection in the mirror and adjust the Rolex on my wrist.

My pressed powder blue suit is perfectly fitted, my face clean-shaven, and I've styled my hair to look effortlessly out of place.

We're high up, but I take the stairs to avoid making awkward conversation in the lift with anyone who recognises me. They've plastered my face over every news network for days, and I want to avoid any questions.

Wearing new loafers straight out of the box wouldn't normally be a problem for me, but they're pinching my toes with each step. I've had to make do with a personal shopper delivery, and I won't be using their services again. The shoes feel like they're a size too small, although the pain gives me something else to focus on.

Once in the lobby, I spot a black car waiting through the glass-windowed front of the building. By its side, a driver built like a lorry checks his phone and taps his foot impatiently. Mother must have given specific instructions to ensure I show up, and he's getting antsy.

"Mr Montgomery." The driver tips his hat in my direction. He breathes a sigh of relief as I approach the car. "I'll be your driver this evening."

"I already have a driver," I reply. "Where's Tim?"

Tim Pope's been on my payroll for years. He's a sensible family man who has got me out of more than one tricky situation, and I trust him.

"Your mother insists I take you." His eyes burn into me to say he'll drag me if I don't abide. "She's paid for Mr Pope to have the night off."

More like she's blackmailed Tim and wants to have her eyes on whatever I'm doing.

"Fine," I say. At least I can drink to get me through whatever tomfoolery she has planned. "Let's go then."

He holds the door open, and I slide inside. We join

the busy London traffic, driving past historical sights and streets bustling with tourists. Their faces glow from the excited rush of seeing the city for the first time. I don't feel the same level of excitement anymore. Instead, I notice how fucking grey everything is. How rubbish drags along the pavement. How homeless people crowd under shop doorways wrapped in sleeping bags, and how everyone's noses are permanently red from the cold. Rain hits the window. Yep, and it's always raining.

We head into Chelsea, unsurprisingly. My mother rarely leaves the borough. Anywhere outside of Zone Two may as well be another continent in her eyes.

I check my phone. No messages. Usually, I'd have something from Callen. A jokey meme to roast me. Failing that, I'd have a random fact from Bram. He liked to send me facts about the local area while he tracked my location. But there's nothing. I stash it away, trying to forget how much the Dukes have changed in a short time. Nothing is the same anymore.

I watch crowds walk past. Suddenly, through the umbrellas, I see a flash of long red hair.

"Stop the car!" I yell. "Now!"

The driver screeches to a halt. "What is it?"

I jump out without explanation and sprint down the street after the woman.

"Out of my way!" I roar, pushing people to the side. She's up ahead. She's wearing a long black coat with the hood pulled up, and red waves escape it. When I reach her, I grab her shoulders and spin her around. "Rose?"

My heart sinks as a stranger looks back. It's not her.

"Sorry," I murmur. The woman looks at me like I'm a crazy mugger. "I thought you were… someone else."

She pulls her bag closer to her side and huffs. Aside from the red hair, there are no similarities.

Fuck, I miss her. All I can think about are her sarcastic quips, determined gaze, eyes that light up when she laughs, and how her soft curves feel in my hands. I'm even seeing her in my dreams.

My shoulder slouch as I get back into the car again.

"Is everything—"

"Keep driving," I snap. "Mother wouldn't want me to be late."

My yearning for Rose isn't all that keeps me up at night. I wonder whether she ran from the ball after discovering what Callen forced her to do or whether she was running from us. Callen's actions showed her that we're monsters. I can't blame her for wanting to get away. Although, it doesn't make it any less painful.

"We're almost there, sir," the driver says.

Ralph didn't give me any clues about the evening, but I can guarantee I'd prefer spending my time disposing of a body.

We reach a row of popular restaurants where celebrities dine. The paparazzi gather around the entrance to one of them. Their cameras are poised, ready to clamber over each other to get the best shot, like hyenas fighting over a carcass. Contrary to popular belief, the paps don't often show up uninvited. The official Royal photographer stands at the front, confirming that they're waiting for me.

"This is your stop, Mr Montgomery."

We park, and the driver gets out to open my door, ready to present me like a debutante at her first ball. Tim would never have done this. He'd always drive around the back of a building to avoid making a scene and drawing any attention to me. He respected my privacy.

I swing one leg out of the car and am blinded by the explosion of lights thrust into my face. Blurry orbs swim before my eyes. People stop to stare, pointing and talking loudly to their friends about the headlines.

*"Look, it's him!"*

*"The Rebel Royal."*

*"Talk about royalty behaving badly."*

Some papers have published more sympathetic stories, but they're even worse than the scandalous ones. Journalists discuss the psychological trauma caused by the fire. If they knew it was a bomb, they'd have a field day. I press my lips together, keeping my expression neutral as I wade through the cameras.

I make it into the restaurant, flanked by my driver-turned-security. I don't need a fucking babysitter, but I have to keep my cool. Some of the businesses I've been trying to invest in have gone cold, and I need them… especially with the state of the Dukes.

Once inside, the thick oak door seals away the chaos. It's the kind of restaurant where it takes months to get a reservation, but the food is subpar, and people only come because it's the place to be seen. The hostess at the desk smiles. My arrival was not a surprise.

"Mr Montgomery, it's so good to see you again," she gushes. "Your date is already waiting."

My cheeks flush with anger. "My… what?"

"Your mother said you have to stay for at least an hour," my new driver hisses in my ear, pre-empting my imminent plan to escape.

"Do you want me to take your jacket?" the over-friendly hostess on the desk offers.

"I'm fine," I hiss.

"I'll take you to your table," she says, well-accustomed

to smiling through rudeness from their clientele. "This way."

She escorts me through the restaurant. At the very least, I'll eat something other than takeaways and meal deals. I expect to be seated somewhere in the back of the restaurant, but I'm not so lucky. The table is in front of the giant bay window to give the paps a perfect view, and my date is already waiting…

# CHAPTER 16
## CALLEN

Finding Seb and Freddie's location was a stroke of luck. I know about Seb's other properties in London, and it just so happened that I struck lucky on my second hit. I don't believe in the universe having your back bullshit, but maybe I'll be a convert to that woo-woo if things keep going my way.

I have no plans to crash their pity party, but keeping tabs on what they're up to doesn't hurt.

I watch Seb leave the building. He's scrubbed up well in an over-priced suit. A posh car is waiting for him. He must be going out on official family business. There's no sign of Freddie, however. I haven't seen him venture outside at all. Seb's the one who goes to the door to collect takeaway deliveries and do their food shopping.

I put my helmet back on and decide to follow the car. I'm cautious—weaving through the traffic behind them and staying a few cars back. I worry that he sees me after he chased a random woman down the street like a man possessed, but he's too deflated when he discovers it's not Rose to notice.

When he arrives at his final destination, the paparazzi descend on him like a group of single mums preying on a newly divorced dad in the playground. I park and hang in the shadows, pressing my back against the wall, and watch him step inside.

It's a pretentious place. Not one I'd go to. Chips wrapped in newspaper with lashings of salt and vinegar beats caviar on bruschetta or whatever bullshit they serve.

Through the window, I watch him move through the restaurant. The waitress guides him to a table to sit with a woman I don't recognise. Her subtle black dress would cost a tenner in Primark but must be designer, and she has a face you'd want to slap. This must be someone off Margaret Montgomery's list of suitors.

If she thinks matching Sebastian with a suitable lass will sort out his problems, she's wrong. Most of Seb's issues come from being part of her toxic family.

I'm about to hop back on the bike and grab a pint at the nearest pub when someone else catches my attention. A car at the opposite end of the street with bullet-proof windows stops, and a woman's tanned leg slides out. She strolls around to speak to the driver, giving me time to check out her arse. Not bad.

My jaw sets when she turns around. How could I forget a pretty face I'd held in a headlock? Bingo, I've found a Killers Club lead.

I'm careful and keep my distance from Blondie, but I don't let her out of my sight. Instead of entering, she detours around the paparazzi, talking on a phone loudly to blend in and prove she belongs there. She's good, maybe even better than Rose.

I could go inside and warn Seb about an assassin crashing his date, but who am I to ruin his quality time with his future wife who resembles a horse? Besides, the Dukes made it clear they didn't want my help by throwing me out of the group.

I bow my head as the car passes to do a loop around the building. They can't see me here twice. I climb onto my bike and drive along, following Blondie's route. She takes a corner down the side of the restaurant. The sneaky bitch wants to slip inside. Maybe she wants to poison Seb or leave him a message.

While the car continues to do a lap, I make a mental note of the plate while Blondie disappears into the back of the restaurant. All I have to do now is wait for her to leave and see where they go to see if they lead me to her.

*I'm coming for you, Rose.*

# CHAPTER 17

SEB

groan inwardly as Beatrice stands to greet me, side-eyeing the flashing cameras to ensure they're watching. I should have known…

"I'm glad you could make it," she says.

Beatrice is still in mourning. Her hair is fixed in a bun, and she's wearing a black, demure dress with a pearl necklace. Although, the happy glint in her eyes tells me she's already done with her grief. Her father's death is the best thing that has happened to her. Her mother died years ago, and she's an only child, so she's set to inherit a fortune.

I stroll over stiffly like a Lego man. I kiss both her cheeks like I'm supposed to. Cue blinding explosions fired through the window.

Beatrice lingers a little longer than necessary before pulling away. She deliberately rests her hand on my arm and whispers seductively, "It *really* is good to see you again."

That'll give the paps the intimate shot they've been waiting for. To my mum's credit, this is a brilliant PR stunt.

What better way to correct my public image than being photographed on a date with a woman whose father died in the fire on the night I disgraced myself?

She waits for me to hold out her chair. I do it grudgingly, then take a seat. A waitress appears out of nowhere, buzzing around us like a fly around shit.

I gesture at the curtains. "Can we shut them?"

I'm not being watched like a zoo animal for an entire meal. Beatrice's face falls. Thankfully, the waitress doesn't see her disappointment.

"Of course, sir," she says, eager to please.

Before they close, Beatrice's hand shoots across the table to snatch mine like a Hungry Hippo. Her touch burns my fingers, and I fight the urge to recoil. To an outsider, we're sharing a meaningful moment. The paps go wild. That's the money shot.

To avoid embarrassing her and facing the wrath of the press, I don't move until the curtains are closed, then I yank my hand out of her clammy grasp. She purses her lips. Did she think a dead daddy would warrant a pity fuck? She reeks of over-priced perfume and desperation.

"Let's get something straight," I say as soon as the waitress is out of our earshot. "I only came tonight because my mother gave me no choice."

"I thought…" She looks down at her lap. I'd almost feel bad if she hadn't socially engineered PDA for the front pages. "I thought that…"

"I'm sorry, Beatrice." I sigh, leaning back in my chair. "I don't know what you've been told, but this isn't a good time for me."

"I'm not having a good time either, if you haven't noticed," she snaps. This is a refreshing change from her usual tendency to agree with everything like a lovesick puppy. "Not everything is about you, Sebastian. I know what you think of me and our world. How you think you're too good for us." Her face contorts into an ugly snarl, erasing any sympathy I may have had. "You need to think of your family and how things look."

The waitress returns to pour our wine and asks, "Can I take your order?"

Beatrice's fake simpering smile returns. "Surprise us," she declares.

I raise my eyebrows. Maybe her father's death has changed her after all.

"You won't be disappointed," the waitress says, bowing her head before scampering away.

"If you knew I didn't want to come tonight, why are you here?" I ask, taking a cautious sip of my red wine.

"Your mother is very persuasive," she says. "And she promised me an engagement ring. From you."

I almost choke. "You do realise that marriage is about what two people want, don't you?"

"We both know that's not how it works. No one marries for love," she says in a snotty tone that makes me cringe. "Your mother thinks you need someone to keep you on track. Someone like me. Someone about to come into a lot of money with the influence and connections you need. Our marriage makes sense. You get stability, and I get a title."

I clench my fists under the table. Her air of entitlement reminds me of my time at university and the girls who lined up to fuck me because of my title. They didn't care about me or who I was. They only wanted to say a royal cock had knighted them.

"I'm not marrying you," I hiss. "Over my dead body."

My mother and Beatrice would love to trap me in a

loveless marriage. They don't care about emotions or that I'm in love with someone else. A woman who I can't stop thinking about.

"You can't escape destiny," Beatrice says. "None of us can."

"If you'll excuse me."

My chair scrapes across the floor as I rise from the table. Beatrice opens her mouth to say something, but I ignore her and storm to the bathroom.

Anger clouds my vision as I stand in front of the sink. I splash my face with cold water, hoping that I'll wake up from a nightmare, but no such luck. I stare at my reflection in the mirror, trying to psych myself up to go out there again. All I've got to do is get through the rest of the evening. The sooner I get this over with, the better.

As I leave, another woman rushes from the Ladies at the same time and walks straight into my chest.

"Shit, I'm sor—" I start to apologise, but my words get caught in my throat when I see who it is.

The blonde blinks up at me in confusion. "Seb?"

"Bethany?" I gawp at Rose's housemate. Freddie sent security to Rose's last known address when we were at the safe house, but it was abandoned. There was no sign of Rose or Bethany anywhere. "What're you doing here?"

"What does it look like?" She plants her hands on her hips. I can see why she and Rose get on. They're both fiery. "But I could ask you the same question..." She looks pointedly at Beatrice across the restaurant, and her expression turns stormy. "Are you on a date?"

"It's not what it looks like," I blurt out. Girls have their friends' backs. Gossip spreads like wildfire. Rose can't think that I'm out with someone else. "Let me exp—"

"It looks like Rose was right to ghost you."

That must mean they've spoken lately.

"Do you know where she is?" I ask. "I need to speak to her."

"Hell fucking no!" Bethany shakes her head. "I don't know what happened between you, but I know she's not been the same since she returned to London. We had to move house. You don't do that unless something bad happened."

"Please, Bethany," I beg. I'll get down on my knees if I have to. "Just tell her I want to talk. I have to explain. I want to make things right."

"By going out with another woman?" She raises her eyebrows in disapproval. "Real smooth, Romeo."

"This is nothing. It's all a set-up for the cameras," I insist. "I care about Rose. I understand that she doesn't want to see me, but things have changed. I have to talk to her—even if it's just for one last time. After that, if she never wants to speak to me again, I'll honour that."

"I won't let you hurt her."

"I'd never hurt her." I ruffle around in my jacket pocket for a card with my number on it. Rose will have lost it along with her phone when Callen threw her bag out of the car. "Give her this. That's all I ask."

Bethany snatches it from me and sniffs in disapproval. "I'll consider it."

Suddenly, Beatrice is behind her. She sizes Bethany up like they're bitter rivals.

"Is there a problem?" Beatrice asks, practically baring her teeth.

Bethany smirks. "Not that I can see, babe."

"Go sit down. I'll be back in a minute," I encourage her, hoping this won't blow my chances of speaking to Rose. "Bethany's an old friend. We're catching up."

"Fine," Beatrice agrees, but can't resist adding, "You can sell yourself elsewhere, *babe*."

Bethany's nostrils flare. "What a keeper," she comments at Beatrice's retreating figure. "If you'll excuse me, I'm just leaving, but I have to make a special request to the kitchen first."

I should follow her. Bethany's our best lead, but Beatrice is waving me over to speak to the official royal reporter who has conveniently appeared at our table. They can't see me chasing after another woman.

I call Freddie. I can't follow her, but he can—if he acts quickly enough. No answer. I hit re-dial. Na-dah. *Shit!* I want to slam my fists into the wall. I try to ring four more times, but he doesn't pick up. He'll be too busy looking for an answer to why Rose abandoned us at the bottom of a whisky bottle. He needs to pull himself together. He's the leader of the Dukes—well, he's supposed to be…

I have no other choice now. All I can do is wait and hope Rose will call.

# CHAPTER 18

## SEB

Beatrice sits straighter in her seat when I return. Her tightly clasped hands resting in front of her on the table as she tries to control her rising anger. "Was she really an old friend?"

"That's none of your business," I reply, then flash her a charming smile. "Just sit and look pretty. That's why you're here, isn't it?"

My phone buzzes, and I jump at it, ignoring Beatrice's tutting. If it's Freddie, there could still be time… nope.

My heart sinks at seeing a text from my mother. The crushing disappointment is worse than the time she interrupted my first blowjob.

> I bought a ring for you. Your driver has
> the box.

My driver catches my eye from the other end of the restaurant. He nods and taps his chest pocket. My eyes narrow. I ignore Beatrice's objections and storm over to him.

"I believe you have something for me," I demand, holding my hand out.

"Of course, sir," he says smoothly, handing it over.

Beatrice's beady eyes burn into my back. She'll know what it is. I'd guess Mum has even shown it to her in advance—hell, they might have even gone ring shopping together.

I shield it from her view and open it. *Holy fuck.* A gigantic, dazzling diamond glitters from inside the velvet box. Glistening sapphires sparkle around the stone. The ring is fit for a queen, not for the claw of a greedy social climber like Beatrice.

I snap the box shut and stash it in my pocket. The ring won't see the light of day again tonight. When, and if, I marry, I'll choose love. Not obligation.

She texts again.

You know what to do.

I ignore her. This is typical. Like most other royals, she's tried to control every aspect of my life since childhood, but this is a step too far—even for her.

When I sit down again, Beatrice is busy flicking through social media on her phone. A smug smirk crosses her face as she admires the photographs of us together filling up her feed. News travels fast in the digital age. Too fast.

Her expression sours when she sees me. "You could at least pretend you're enjoying yourself."

Rose was the last woman I took out to dinner. During our date, I had excited butterflies in my stomach, sweaty palms from nervous anticipation, and was filled with worry about whether I was fucking it up. That's the feeling I want to have.

"Here are your starters." The waiter provides a reprieve, appearing with two soup bowls. "Wild truffle and smoked mushroom for you, Mr Montgomery. Tomato for—"

"I don't like mushrooms," I interrupt. I'm acting like a dick, and I know it.

"That's fine, darling," Beatrice steps in to temper my rudeness and dazzle him with a smile that resembles a gurning chihuahua. "We can swap."

I don't try the dish, dragging my spoon through the bowl to pass the time. They forced me to be here, but I don't have to enjoy it.

"Aren't you enjoying your soup?" Beatrice says, daintily sipping the liquid off the spoon like we're having high tea.

I push the bowl away. "I'm not hungry."

I check my watch. How many more courses do I have to endure?

After she's finished, Beatrice dabs the corners of her mouth, then burps. My eyes widen in surprise, and I snort. Her cheeks turn a flaming red.

I raise my eyebrows. "What would my mother say?"

She jumps up from the table, holding the napkin to her mouth. "Excuse me, I…"

She races through the restaurant to the bathroom, shoving a few people out of her way to get there quicker.

I guess it's a good thing I had no appetite.

# CHAPTER 19
## CALLEN

Her hair flows behind her like golden ribbons as she leaves the restaurant. No one would guess the hot blonde is a bloodthirsty assassin… and the bitch will lead me straight to Rose.

*Not long now, princess.* My cock twitches in excitement. *I'm coming for you.* I won't have to deal with Freddie acting as a guard dog or Seb whining in my ear. I'll find the woman who can bring all my fantasies to life—the woman who has made it impossible to get hard for anyone else—and make her mine.

I don't rev too hard, avoiding drawing any unnecessary attention. I kick off from the road while Blondie hops back into the black car, and they set off.

Judging by no immediate sirens, I assume Seb's still alive, but I'm not sticking around to make sure. There's no point—if she wanted him dead, it'd already be too late to save him.

I know London roads like the back of my hand. I'm familiar with the city's impatient drivers, angry beeping, and the cries of 'move, wanker!' through open windows. As much as I like the remote Scottish Highlands, the capital has its charm.

I weave through the streets, travelling by back roads to avoid being seen while keeping them in my vision. They're not driving erratically or taking strange turns like they know I'm following, but I can't take any chances. I know better than that.

When I worked for Torean, he sent me on various run-around jobs: tailing people, collecting evidence, and delivering punishments. My vehicle of choice then was a black cab that helped me blend in.

*Where are you going, Blondie?*

We pass the pub where I saw Rose and her agent pal the night we fucked for the first time. We're close to the Dukes' base now. The Killers Club has been right under our noses all along.

The traffic lights change to red as I reach the front of the queue. I watch their car stop outside a townhouse.

I can't lose them, but I'll bet their place is hooked into more cameras than Scotland Yard. They can't catch wind that I'm onto them. I decide to do a loop and see whether they are still there on my return. Losing them is a risk, but I follow my gut.

A twisted grin spreads over my face when I come back to see they haven't moved.

*I've got you.*

Blondie and her tattooed boyfriend, who I had the pleasure of meeting outside the Conservatory, are oblivious to my presence. They stroll into the house together without a care in the world.

They think they're the predators, but they're being

hunted. Tracking them down wasn't as difficult as I expected it to be. All I had to do was get rid of the dead weight holding me back…

# CHAPTER 20

## IVY

Bram is holding back, refusing to comply. Two days have passed, and all he's done is write brief notes. A few sentences at best. He's told me nothing I don't already know about the Dukes. When will Alaric take me off babysitting duty and give me a proper job?

I sigh, wondering how many more hours I'm going to waste down here. Thankfully, Bram has been given fresh clothes and permission to wash regularly, so I'm spared the misfortune of being around someone who reeks.

"Look," I try to bargain with him, "you're going to need to give me more than that."

He slides a note underneath the door. It's a lovely drawing of a cock and balls, complete with throbbing veins and a drop of cum spurting from the tip.

"Real fucking mature," I retort, screwing it up and hurling it down the corridor. "You're not taking me seriously."

I can't see him, but I imagine he's snickering. I stand and open the hatch to look into his cell. He's leaning against the brick wall casually. Since he's been here, his dark hair has grown, and he's sporting a beard. It suits him. His muscled arms flex as he turns in my direction. They're covered in traditional tattoos that have faded from many hours spent in the sun, but it makes them look like part of his skin instead of colourful stickers. The owl around his neck holds him in a permanent chokehold.

I imagine my hands smothering the owl as Bram's lips curve into a mischievous grin. He gets happier the more annoyed I get. At least one of us is having a good time.

"If you haven't noticed, you're a fucking prisoner," I hiss. "Do you want me to take you back to the torture room again?" I look at his hands and the nail beds, still recovering from my last attack. "I can tear off more of your fingernails quicker than a wax strip."

He shrugs and extends his arms, wiggling his fingers in my direction as if to say *be my guest.*

"Alaric was right to cut out your tongue." I scowl. "You sure are a sarcastic fucker."

His green-yellow cat-like eyes sparkle through the dim light back at me and narrow. *So I've been told*, they seem to say. Although he's trying to challenge me, I see something hiding behind his stare—pain, trauma, and stories that he'll never be able to tell.

As he steps forward, my gaze involuntarily strays to the bulge in his grey tracksuit bottoms. *Jesus, he's hung!* I jerk my eyes away. He's gorgeous, but he's a mark. A mark that should be dead.

"You're infuriating," I huff, slamming the hatch closed. "You're not the only one who can give the silent treatment."

I say nothing as the minutes stretch on. I hear him

moving around, but I won't give him the satisfaction of checking what he's doing.

Suddenly, the door flies open at the end of the corridor. Stephanie totters towards me in ridiculously high heels. It's a miracle she hasn't broken an ankle wearing those skyscrapers.

"Have you been shopping again?" I ask, checking out the gorgeous skin-tight powder blue dress that hugs her perfect figure.

"Not shopping," she says, "but I have been out for a bite to eat…"

I raise my eyebrows at her tone. "Is that code for something else?"

"Look who I saw." She thrusts her phone into my hands to show me a photograph of a dimly lit restaurant.

I see a couple sitting at a table. She points at them, and my chest feels like it's been hit by a train. *Seb?* I pinch my fingers and drag them across the screen to get a better look at the woman with a shit-eating grin sitting opposite him. I've already blown her daddy's arms off, and now I'm overcome with the urge to blast Beatrice's hands off her dainty wrists too.

"Did he see you?" I ask coldly, not giving anything away.

"Yes," she replies, pausing to check whether I'll ask more questions, but I decided against it. "We had a chat. He was asking about you."

I shrug like it means nothing, although I want to know what he said. I don't know why seeing them together annoys me so much. It shouldn't. Seb made his feelings for her clear at the party—unless it was all an act. I can't trust anything the Dukes told me. Seb has been living a double life long enough that lying comes as naturally to him as breathing. It takes a liar to know one.

"He wants you to call him." Stephanie tilts her head and takes a card out of her bag, but she doesn't hand it over. "Maybe you should. Not yet. But it's a good backup option for us."

"I guess."

"Come on, Ivy." Her voice sends a shiver down my spine. "Don't you want to see Mr Hot Cute Dimples again? Maybe you should get one last hoorah."

"That's Alaric's decision," I say, playing it safe.

"Let me speak to him." She winks, pocketing the card again. "I don't think we should wait for the Dukes to come to us. We should go to them."

She rarely disagrees with Alaric's decisions, so her voicing an opposing opinion puts me on edge. I don't know her game plan, but something isn't right.

"I'll see you later." She nudges her head at Bram's cell. "And good luck making him talk."

"I'll be waiting a lifetime for that," I mutter.

I sit down again. A few minutes later, Bram slides a note under the door.

*Are you okay?*

I snort. "I've never been fucking better."

Haven't I?

# CHAPTER 21
## FREDDIE

stand under the shower spray, letting the hot water trail over my muscles and trickle down my abs. Steam fills the room; the temperature is intolerably hot, and the humidity makes my breathing heavy. This is the place I think best.

I've languished in a bottomless pit of despair for days, but I have to pull myself out of it. This isn't like five years ago when I saw evidence of a car wreckage that I was sure no one could survive. Rose is alive, likely terrified, and questioning who the fuck she is after what Callen forced her to do… and I need to find her. I need to be the one who lifts her up and puts her back together because she's the woman who completes me.

In my head, I go over the little details in the days leading up to the ball. I've combed through every conversation Rose and I had to see if I'm missing something.

Spencer lied about knowing her over the phone. Now we're back in London; I need to see him again. If we learn more about Rose and her past, we have a higher chance of finding where she is now.

I printed out the photograph of him and Rose, tore it in half and kept only her face. It's the only decent photo of her I have. I put it in a golden frame. A reminder whenever I wake up of why I'm doing this, and what I have to lose.

Her face doesn't look the same now, though. Her nose and jaw are a different shape after her injuries from the accident, but it proves she's rebuilt herself once. She's strong, and I can help her do it again.

I raise my head to the water, splashing my face and scrubbing my neck. I recall her soft lips tugging on my ear in the throes of passion, and the tickle of her pointed tongue. My cock hardens instantly, throbbing at the thought. I can't help it. Thinking of how her body fits so perfectly against mine drives me wild.

I haven't touched myself since we fucked, but I can't resist now. I take my cock in my fist, letting the shower lash down on my back like a scorching whip. I shut my eyes, remembering how I took her hardened nipples in my mouth. Her back arched, showing me how much she liked it. I can still taste her sweetness gushing over my tongue, feel the warmth of being drenched in her juices, and see how good her pussy looked filled with my cum. I grunt as I recall pushing my cum back inside her, wanting to keep it there. Wanting… wanting… *Fuck*.

I use my spare hand to steady myself on the slippery tiles to stop myself from losing balance. Her wet pussy was so tight when it hugged my cock, her moans sending vibrations racing through my body, and I badly wanted to hear them now.

I imagine her. I imagine my cock disappearing inside her and thrusting so deeply that I set up home and don't let go. My hand pumps harder, quickening my pace, more urgent and needy.

"Mine," I grunt. My hips shudder. "All fucking mine."

Because she is. All fucking mine. My cum spills over my hands as I reel from the memories.

Rose isn't a woman I'll let go. She's the woman I want to spend my life with. The woman I want to fill with cum again and again until her belly swells with my growing child. This isn't just a relationship I'm trying to hold onto. We may not have spent much time together, but I can feel it in my bones that she's my one. The woman who was made for me. She's my entire fucking life.

I turn the water ice cold and finish showering with haste, baptised in a renewed clarity and hunger for finding her.

I grab a towel and wrap it around my middle. As soon as I do, the door to the bathroom bursts open, and Seb appears.

"You could have kn—"

"I've been trying to call you," he blasts. His expression is thunderous.

"What happened?" I ask sharply. "What is it?"

His eyes are alight with fire and an optimism I haven't seen for days. "It's Rose."

"Did you see her?" My heart races. "Is she here?"

I half-expect her to be standing behind him with her confident grin and beckon me to join her in bed with her little finger. I should never have let her leave my side.

"I saw her friend, Bethany, at the restaurant," Seb explains. "She's spoken to Rose."

"Is she okay? What did she say?" I bark questions at him. "I need you to tell me everything."

"From what she said, Rose seems to be okay." Seb runs

his fingers through his hair, shifting his weight from one foot to the other. "But Bethany was mad. Rose hasn't told her anything, but it sounds like she's messed up after what happened."

"Fucking Callen," I growl, directing my anger at the no-good piece of shit I let into our lives because I thought he deserved a second chance.

Torean, Callen's twin, is a fucking monster. When I met Callen in a pub, I saw potential in him… and this is how he repays me? He's turned the woman I love into a killer! Rose is strong, projecting to the world she doesn't care, but I see the real her. Someone who is inherently good, and Callen has tainted that.

"I asked Bethany to give Rose my number," Seb says. "She might call."

"You didn't follow her?" I demand. "How could you have let this chance slip away?"

"What could I do? Chase her while surrounded by the paparazzi?" Seb snarls. "I tried calling you, but it kept going to voicemail." Guilt stabs at my stomach. I've screwed up. Again. I let her get away. "But this is good news, isn't it? It's progress."

"It's a lead," I say, strolling to my bedroom to change. "But we still need to follow up on another one."

Seb frowns. "You don't mean…"

"We're going to pay the Bexley mansion a visit."

This time, we're getting the truth.

# CHAPTER 22

## BRAM

The rough brick digs into my spine. She takes gulps of air, trying to steady her breathing. Did hearing about Seb being with another woman bother her? I push a blank sheet of paper under the door to prompt her as a friendly nudge.

"What're you trying to do?" Her sassy voice pipes up again. "Give me a paper cut?"

If she wasn't the psycho bitch responsible for the fresh scar burned into my chest, I'd say she had a good sense of humour.

I scrawl my next message.

*How are they?*

The paper disappears. I hear it crinkle as she crushes it in her hand. She knows who I'm talking about instantly. The atmosphere changes, growing more tense, and the air thickens. Does that mean she genuinely cares about them?

I didn't think she was capable of feeling anything—at least, not anymore.

"How am I supposed to know how they are?" she snaps. "You're not the only one being kept prisoner inside this fucking building."

I take a risk.

I slide it under. Maybe this will make her blow up. That's what I've been pushing her to do. I've been giving her nothing in the hope that she'll lose her temper and open the door to beat the shit out of me.

I hear my note being ripped apart and shredded into tiny pieces.

"You don't know what you're talking about." She sounds mad, but her tone has softened slightly—only enough for someone like me to detect. "If you want to talk about the Dukes so much, why don't you tell me how you became one of them?"

I exhale deeply, hovering the pen over the paper. Where do I start?

"Let me guess, you won't tell me," she answers. "Why don't we cut the bullshit, Bram? Do you think Alaric will let me sit down here forever, waiting for you to give me information? You're dead weight. It won't be long before he cuts you loose."

Not unless he cuts her loose first…

I write a message.

*If I'm never going to talk, why keep asking me questions?*

"Smart arse." I can hear her smile. "If you won't tell me

why you joined the Dukes, why don't you tell me why you stayed with them for so long? In the army, you followed orders. Why did you want to go back to following someone else after what happened? After what you did."

My heartbeat quickens, and a cold sweat breaks over my brow. How does she know about that? Unless…

"You're not the only person who can use a computer to dig into someone's past." She reads my thoughts, mocking me now. "Do you think about all those innocent people you killed?"

I grab the paper. The pen nib almost tears straight through it, turning the question around on her.

*Do you think about what you've done? The people you've killed?*

She laughs like a maniac. The sassy woman with a dark sense of humour is gone, and the monster stands in her place. The agent they've turned her into. "I kill people who deserve it."

I write:

*Do the Dukes deserve it?*

"Why don't you tell me?" she presses. "Are they evil men who deserve to die?"

I snort and reply.

*You should know.*

*You're the one fucking them.*

"Fuck you."

We're going in circles like two hungry predators picking pieces off a dead carcass. I write another message.

*You asked me if I think about them—the people I killed.*
*I don't want to, but I can't stop it.*
*Sometimes I can't stop the thoughts.*

"I know the feeling," she grumbles, but I suspect she's not talking about her marks now.

Maybe we've got more in common than I first thought. I change tact. She's shown a shred of vulnerability. I could use that to work a different angle—all I need is something, like a password to a locked computer, to get inside her head.

*Do you think about what Spencer did?*

She jumps from her sitting position and peers through the window to my cell. Her wild eyes, glistening with fury, sear into me but show something else. Pain. So much fucking pain.

"Do you think this is a joke?" she sneers. "My sister died. Spencer murdered her. Do I think about what he did? Of course, I fucking do. Every minute of every day. I think about how I'm going to make him pay."

She slams it shut and storms away, swearing under her breath.

*Shit!* I throw the plastic water bottle at the wall. It bounces straight back, not giving me the same satisfying feeling as throwing something breakable.

How am I supposed to get through to her when neither of us will open up? She's impossible.

# CHAPTER 23
## FREDDIE

"Remind me why we're back here again?" Seb asks, glancing at the security guards swarming outside Bexley's mansion further down the street.

"Because we're here to get answers," I reply. "The truth this time."

"He won't speak to us," Seb says. "Don't you remember what he said on the phone? He made his intentions clear, and if you haven't forgotten, we're unarmed."

I wave my hand to silence him, then raise my finger to point at a moving figure. "There she is."

He follows my gaze to watch Spencer's elderly housekeeper head out of the staff entrance and hobble down the street towards where we're parked. Her schedule runs like clockwork.

Seb clears his throat nervously. "You're not going to hurt her, are you?"

"Is that a serious question?" I snap. "No, I'm not going to hurt an old lady. What do you take me for?"

I'm not a total animal. If Callen was here, I couldn't make the same promise.

"I didn't—"

"Shut up," I growl. *Come on, lady—pick up the pace.* We should wait until she's out of the eyeshot of the mansion before approaching her. Spencer's guards don't look twice at the old dear, but they'll come running if she screams bloody murder. "She's worked for Spencer for years. Staff always know everything that's going on, and Spencer lied to us about Rose before. She'll know the truth, and we need her to talk."

The woman trundles by opposite us. I put the car into gear and follow, slowing to a crawl at her side. I lower the window. Seb can do the rest. He's charming enough to talk most people into doing whatever he wants. He hasn't even opened his mouth when she takes one look at him and hisses, "I'm not speaking to you."

"All we want is five minutes," Seb bargains.

"You're wasting your time," she says.

Her wrinkled lips purse, almost disappearing into her face, and she keeps walking.

"All we want to do is ask you a few questions," Seb reasons. "Then you'll never hear from us again."

"You don't work for Mr Bexley anymore," she says. She's loyal to the man who treats her worse than a dog, unwilling to jeopardise her pension so close to the finish line. "I've got nothing to say."

We continue to follow her. She tries to hurry, but her swollen ankles slow her down.

"We just want to know one—"

"Show her," I interrupt him. "Show her the picture."

"Can you tell us whether you recognise this woman?"

Seb holds up his phone to show her the photograph of Rose and Spencer.

She freezes, even as her gaze softens. She knew her—even liked her—then the walls crashed down.

Her eyes narrow in suspicion. "What's this about?"

I slam on the brakes. Seb's gentle approach failed, so it was my turn to step in.

"You've been talking to someone in a moving car. What would Spencer think if he found out? We all know his paranoia is getting worse." I take no joy in frightening her, but she bites her lip, weighing her options and knowing I'm right. "We'll give you a lift home, okay? All we want to know is who she is."

She hesitates, glancing back over her shoulder, then makes a harumphing noise before getting into the back-seat. We drive for a few minutes before coming to a stop. She fidgets, growing more anxious as time passes.

Seb turns to ask, "So, you know her?"

The woman nods. Her hands tremble as she clutches onto her bag tightly.

"What's all this about?" she asks. "Why are you dragging up the past? All of this happened years ago."

"How did Spencer know her?" I demand.

She shifts under my scrutiny.

"She was his girlfriend before..." The woman drops her voice. "The accident."

"A car crash?"

"Were they happy?" Seb butts in.

"Mr Bexley was," she replies. "Well, they both were at the start, and then..."

"What happened?" I press.

"I've said enough." She shakes her head. "Why are you

asking about what happened to that poor girl? It doesn't matter to anyone now."

"It matters to us," I reply fiercely. "You said they were both happy at the start. What happened after that?"

"She moved into the mansion early on," she recalls wistfully. "She was kind, even helped me clean up sometimes. I thought he'd finally found someone who could help him. Someone he could settle down with, you know? Besotted with her, he was. He doted on her. But Mr Bexley loved her too much."

We all know that's code for him being a possessive, controlling bastard.

"What did he do?" Seb asks gently. "We won't tell anyone. Everything you say stays in this car."

"She couldn't stand it anymore, his rules and tempers, so she left him after they had a big argument," she says. "She waited until he left and snuck out of the staff entrance. Mr Bexley was furious when he found out. I've never seen him so angry. Not long after that… a week maybe… they found the car and those two girls."

My head spins. It doesn't make sense. Rose told us Matteo Santiago was responsible for her sister's death.

"I told Mr Bexley I wanted to go to the funeral." She sniffs and dabs her eyes. "The only time I ever stood up to him, that was. But it didn't happen. Neither of those girls had a funeral. No family to pay for it. Ivy deserved better than that."

Seb cocks his head to the side. "Ivy?"

"Yes." Her brow dips in confusion. "Ivy Penrose. The girl in the photo you showed me. That's her name."

"Not Daisy?" Seb asks.

"Daisy was her sister, I think, but I never met her," she

says. "No, that's definitely Ivy, alright. I'll never forget her face."

"Thank you," I reply smoothly, taking out my wallet and pulling out a stack of notes. "You've been very helpful."

She snatches the money and stuffs it inside her purse. Before getting out, she delivers a warning. "Don't go bringing up the past. I don't know why you're asking about Ivy Penrose after all this time, but if you know what's good for you, you'll leave it alone. Mr Bexley is a powerful man." She clambers from the car. "You shouldn't come here again."

She doesn't look back, disappearing around the next corner, while realisation dawns on us.

"Why would Rose pretend to be her sister?" Seb murmurs. "She said Matteo, *Ivy's* possessive ex, caused the crash…"

From Seb's expression, I can tell he's thinking the same. What if Matteo wasn't the jealous lover she referred to in her story? What if it was really Spencer? If we believe what she told us, there were multiple people involved. People that she'd have a grudge against.

"Do you think Rose could be the Killers Club client wanting Spencer's men dead?" I ask, daring to vocalise my suspicions aloud.

"She could be," Seb agrees. "It makes sense. Whoever wants them dead holds a serious grudge."

Suddenly, Seb's phone rings. He answers it. He doesn't speak for long, only a few abrupt sentences, but the colour drains from his face as he talks.

"That was my brother," he explains after ending the call. "He's got more news about the Collingsbrook fire. They found another dead body. It got shielded from the bulk of the blast under collapsing rubble, and the coroner's first inspection thinks that strangulation might have been the cause of the death."

"So there was a murder that night." Dread makes my stomach flip. The Collingsbrook Ball is turning into an Agatha Christie novel more with each day. "Who died?"

"Graham Baldwin."

"Graham Baldwin…" I scratch my chin. "Why does that name sound familiar?"

Then, it hits me.

His name came up during our research into Spencer Bexley. Graham used to work for him, like the other men who have died recently.

*No, surely not…*

Questioning one thing makes you question everything, and then pieces start to slot together where they didn't before. My mind flips back over the past few months, going through the timelines.

*Rose met Seb at the party where we suspected Danny's killer poisoned him.*

*I saw Rose at the bar at the same time we were due to meet the Killers Club.*

*She was at the Collingsbrook Ball—a high-security event that usually never lets outsiders in.*

There are too many coincidences.

"What if Rose didn't hire the Killers Club?" I turn to Seb. "What if Rose is *in* the Killers Club?"

And we've been too fucking blind to see it.

# CHAPTER 24

## IVY

"I'm not going back there," I tell Alaric. I walk back and forth, unable to sit still. Being cooped up underground is making me antsy. "He's not opening up to me."

Alaric raises one eyebrow from his chair at Jonathon's bedside.

"Who would want to?" Jonathon croaks. He's making a good recovery and becoming more lucid. Thankfully, his injuries have left no permanent damage. It's a shame getting his head bashed hasn't stopped him from being a pain in my arse.

"You better shut up, or I'll put you into another coma," I snap.

He laughs, but it turns into a cough, making him wince from the pain. I grin smugly. Good, it serves him right.

"Are you letting him win?" Alaric asks. He checks his watch. "By my calculation, you've spent over twelve hours with him, and the best you've got out of him is a drawing of a cock."

Jonathon snickers. He should be careful, or I'll play with his medication and slip arsenic into his drip.

"It's hard to interrogate someone from behind a door," I remind them, "and he can't speak, remember?"

"This is a new challenge for you, Ivy," Alaric says. "You've got something to prove."

"Can't I open the door?" I ask. "It'll be easier to read his facial expression."

"Under no circumstances should you open the door, understood?" He uses his authoritative voice that tells me no amount of arguing will change his mind. "Bram's strong."

I scoff, flicking my hair over my shoulder. "You think he could hurt me?"

"Look at me." Jonathon pipes up. "Let that be a warning."

"But I'm a better fighter," I counter, adding with a sweet smile, "No offence."

Jonathon smirks. "When I get out of this bed, I'll show you—"

"I've seen Bram in the field," Alaric interrupts. "He's strong, and he doesn't know his own strength. You will not open that door. That's an order."

"Fine!" I blow a loose strand of hair out of my face. "But I'm not a psychic. If you want information, why don't you recruit Mystic fucking Meg?"

"I never thought I'd see you giving up." Alaric reclines in his chair. "Has being around royalty gone to your head, and you think you're too good for this job now?"

His teasing infuriates me.

"No one beats me," I spit.

I grab my bag, filled with a big stack of paper, and

march away. I'm returning to the cells. Bram will talk to me. He has to.

"That's my girl," Alaric calls after me. "Don't give up."

"Fuck you," I grumble. "I didn't ask for a motivational speech."

I contemplate the best way to open the conversation as I walk down. How can I get inside Bram's head? How can I make him open up? Alaric must think he has some valuable information to warrant me wasting my time with him.

I take the lift down to HQ's lowest level and hang a right to the dungeon. I open the heavy steel door to the corridor.

Bram's cell is right at the end of the empty rows. He hears me coming and pushes a piece of paper under the door for my arrival.

*I thought you weren't coming back.*

I snap open the hatch. He stands against the back wall of his cell, and I take a few steps back. Alaric told me not to open the door. But, if my back is against the corridor wall and Bram stays in the same spot, we can see each other from the shoulders up when Bram slouches.

I study him. Could he beat me in a fight? He's six foot seven, towering over me, and although he's lost weight since being imprisoned, he hasn't lost any muscle. He must be working out in his cell. He grins and raises his hand in a sarcastic wave. A giant hand that could wrap right around my throat.

"I changed my mind," I say. "What can I say? I like talking to someone who doesn't talk back."

His grin widens. It doesn't seem forced, a genuine

smile that makes crinkles appear at the sides of those magical cat-like eyes. In another life, he is someone I'd check out in a club, but his hotness can't distract me from my mission.

He bends to pick up a sheet of paper, giving me the perfect view of his back muscles and broad shoulders. He turns, leaning against the wall to write, then holds the paper in front of him for me to read.

*I'm sorry about what I said.*

I blink and re-read.

"You're sorry?" I scoff.

My eyes look up from the paper and meet his. Where does he think he is? We're not in *Love Actually*!

He stares back. Electricity fizzles through the air between us. I don't know how long we look at each other, but there's a building tension I don't quite understand.

Finally, I clear my throat. "Good." I don't know what else I can say to his apology, but being my usual snarky bitch self is the safest option. "You should be sorry."

He writes another note, but he doesn't hold it up. When he's done, he folds it in half carefully. My heartbeat quickens as he heads to the open window. I should tell him to back away and post it under the door, but what damage can he do through a tiny gap? Break my pinkie finger?

He thrusts the message through the window like a letterbox and waits for me to retrieve it. I approach cautiously, small steps towards the hulking caged beast. I'm quick, snatching the paper from his hands.

He steps back, a bemused expression flickers over his face like he's asking, *What did you think I was going to do?*

His gaze sears into me as I unfold the message and read his words.

*I'm sorry I couldn't save her.*

I turn away so he can't see my reaction. I won't allow him to see the pain etched over my features that I've been carrying around on my shoulders like a block of lead.

I think back to Daisy that night. How broken she was. How I tried to reach her. How all I wanted was to swap places with her.

Heavy footsteps, crunching twigs, a never-ending tunnel of darkness, a light that pulled back… and a voice. A deep voice that reverberated through my core and made me feel safe. I haven't thought about that voice for years, but now… *Bram.*

It was him. I never saw the face of the man who rescued me, and I'll never hear his voice again. The voice that brought me back from the brink of death.

"I wish you saved her too," I murmur in agreement, then whirl around in accusation. "Why did you come back for me?" He tilts his head, watching me closely. He's searching for something, but I'm not sure what. "You were working for Spencer." I point at him. "You should have left me to die on the side of the road with her!"

He arches one eyebrow. *Is that what you wanted?*

I sigh in exasperation. We're not getting into this. I've never spoken to a therapist because I don't need a clueless person to tell me how I should feel, and I'm not going to start now with a mark—even if he'll inevitably die soon.

"I remember you," I tell him. "I remember your voice."

His eyes widen in genuine surprise.

"Do you regret it now?" I ask, wanting him to agree. Wanting him to let me know how much he hates me because that's what I deserve. I ruin everyone's life who tries to help me. Just look at what happened to Daisy. "Do you regret saving me?"

He shakes his head.

"Why?" I explode. My words ricochet off the empty prison walls, leaving a haunting echo behind. "Spencer would have killed you if he found out. You risked your life for someone you never met and lost your voice because of me!"

He shrugs, looking at his feet.

"Why didn't you tell the Dukes you used to work for Spencer?" I ask. "If you did, maybe they'd have worked out who I was. Why didn't you tell anyone what you did?"

His gaze meets mine with a renewed fire. He grips the pen so tightly that his knuckles turn white. He writes two words.

*For you.*

"For me?" I frown, letting my anger take over. I can deal with anger. Anger is easier. Anger is what's kept me going for five years. Anger keeps me alive. "Because you enjoyed being the saviour? Do you have a hero complex?" My inner bitch rises to the surface, and I mock him, "Does saving people make you hard?"

His jaw sets in fury, and he turns his back on me.

"Do you like the feeling of playing God? Do you want

to be powerful?" I demand. "Is that it? Come on, you can tell me…"

He sits on the floor, so I can't see him anymore. Whatever more profound moment we shared is gone. It's better that way. He slides a message under the door.

*I did it because I wanted to protect you.
I wanted to give you a second chance at life.*

"A life like this?" I laugh coldly. "A life that revolves around killing people? A life with no love and filled with blood?"

He jumps up. A storm brews behind his eyes, making them darken. Accusation hardens his features, from his clenched jaw to balled fists.

He writes hurriedly; his pen jabs through the paper, and each letter ends in sharp points.

*I thought I was taking you somewhere safe. Alaric told me he ran a witness protection programme. I didn't know.*

"Witness protection?" I snort in disbelief. "Yeah, fucking right. You know, it's ironic, considering that's the cover story I told the Dukes. They believed that bullshit, too. You can't expect me to believe you didn't know what Alaric really did?"

His fury slips for a second, and the intensity of his glare makes me squirm. It's filled with sadness, regret, and disappointment… well, shit. Maybe he did have no idea.

I cross my arms. "You truly didn't know?"

He writes again. The ring of yellow around his pupils seems to glow as he thrusts the note through the open hatch. When I take it from him, our fingers brush for a second. His skin scorches mine like I've touched a hot pan, and I jump back. *What the fuck was that?* He springs away like I've burned him with the soldering iron again. *Did he feel it too?*

"Electric shock," I dismiss, swishing my hair over my face as I look down to read the note so he can't see the blush heating my cheeks.

*If I'd known, I'd never have brought you to him.*

"What would you have done then?" I ask. "You worked for a man who tried to kill me. Don't you think he'd have found out if you were harbouring his ex?"

*I resigned the morning after it happened.*

"But that didn't stop the Dukes from working with him," I say, rolling my eyes at his reply. "How can I trust someone who does that?"

His writing becomes a rushed scrawl. He hesitates for a second before holding out the paper for me to take.

*I didn't tell them because I was trying to protect you.*

*Do you think lying and watching Freddie mourn a dead girl was easy?*

*I never told him to keep you safe and protect your new identity.*

I choke back the Gobstopper-sized lump forming in my throat. He's lying. He has to be.

"You must regret saving me now," I say, ending our conversation. "I'll be back later with food."

Before I leave, I shred Bram's words.

No one needs to see them.

# CHAPTER 25

## BRAM

The dungeon door rattles when she returns. Our last conversation still hangs between us like a thick smog. Do I regret saving her? I regret my choice of the person I trusted to protect her. I regret following Alaric's orders and never checking to see how she was doing, but if I could go back in time, I'd still do it again.

That night wasn't only life-changing for Ivy. It proved that I could do something good. That I wasn't just a killing machine. Saving her gave me hope I could make things better rather than cause suffering. It gave me the strength to want to redeem myself. I'll never be able to atone for my sins, but I could protect people too.

Ivy opens the hatch and thrusts a plastic carton through it. A steaming ready meal that's charred around the edges balances precariously on the ledge. Who can burn something in the microwave?

"Sorry." She wrinkles her nose. "I can't cook."

I take it from her anyway, noticing another equally crispy one on the floor for her to eat.

We sit and eat together in silence. I take my time, having to be careful with each mouthful. Choking is a risk for me. I can still taste with the small part of my tongue I have left, but the flavours aren't as strong as they used to be. On the positive side, I have a higher tolerance for spicy food now.

When I've finished eating, I slide a message I wrote earlier underneath the door.

*I don't regret it.*

She draws a sharp intake of breath and scrunches up the paper. "You should."

I reply:

*You never thanked me for saving your life.*

She snorts, seeing the humour in it. Underneath her hard exterior, there's still a person who deserves another chance. Is that the woman Freddie and Seb see when they look at her?

"Thank you, Bram." She stands and peers through the window. Her voice drips with sarcasm, and she rolls her eyes. "I'm ever so grateful."

She watches me write, and I hold it up for her to see.

*There's more to life than killing people.*

"Is there?" She shrugs. "From where I'm standing, that's the best thing about it."

I write:

*Seb and Freddie care about you.*

Her tense jaw twitches. The Ice Queen might care about them, too.

"They don't know me," she says. "I've been doing a job, that's all. When they find out who I am, they'll hate me."

She reminds me of myself five years ago. She thinks she's irredeemable. Maybe that's why she cares about the Dukes. They showed her what her life could be like. Freddie, Seb, and Callen aren't perfect, but the Dukes are a family, or they were…

I take a gamble.

*I think you care about them too.*

"You don't know what you're talking about," she hisses at my latest scrawl as I cross out my words. "The Dukes are a Killers Club target."

I see through her lies and decide to push harder.

*The Dukes can help you.*

"I don't need help," she insists. "What can the Dukes really do? They're still men! Men only care about themselves."

*They're not Spencer.*

"You don't know that," she says, but she's not just talking to me now. "Spencer was charming at the beginning, just like Freddie and Seb. How do I know they're not the same? I'm part of the Killers Club; we have each other's backs, and loyalty comes above all else."

*You're wrong.*

"Wrong?" Her jaw drops. "Don't tell me you're going to spin me some bullshit about how love doesn't only exist in fairytales? This isn't a fucking musical!"

I wasn't going to mention love, but if she has, it must be on her mind. She cares about the Dukes more than she wants to admit to herself.

My hand moves across the page before I change my mind. I'm taking a risk. A risk that not only compromises the mission Alaric gave me but also any prospect of my release.

*The Killers Club isn't as loyal as you think.*

Once she's read it, I rip the paper and stuff the note into my mouth. My spit turns it into a gooey ball, and I swallow it to destroy the evidence.

"Come on, Bram. What're you trying to do? Play mind games with me?" Her deep brown eyes narrow. "It won't work."

I hold her gaze, unblinking, trying to show her how sincere I am. *I'm not lying.*

"Go on then," she encourages. "Hit me with it. Tell me why the Killers Club isn't loyal."

She's deflecting. That's how she keeps people at arm's length when she's scared.

I write the note, then stand and walk over to her, taking slow steps.

When I'm close enough but not within reaching distance, I hold up the tiny note. Her eyes scan it and widen.

*Christopher Trout is one of Alaric's clients.*

I pop the note into my mouth again and swallow it.

"You're lying," she declares, but her voice shakes, weaved with fear. "You're making it up."

I shrug. *Why don't you find out?* She holds my stare like she's trying to scope me out. I hope she sees the warning in mine. *Be careful.*

She storms away, leaving me wondering what the hell she's going to do next. I might have made a terrible mistake…

# CHAPTER 26

IVY

try to keep my erratic heart rate in check, but I feel like I've raided a pick-and-mix counter and downed two litres of fizzy drink from how fast it's going.

Bram must be lying, right? There's no way Alaric would accept Christopher Trout as a client when he knows what Christopher and the others did to me and Daisy that night. Alaric nursed me back to health, shared in my rage, and promised me justice. He'd never take money from a man like that… would he?

"How did it go?" Alaric steps from the training room as I pass by in his athletic gear. His veins protrude from his muscular arms, and he wipes his sweaty face with a towel.

"He's given me nothing useful," I snarl venomously. "I don't know why we're keeping him alive and wasting my time."

Alaric's expression stays unreadable. "Bram might be able to tell us more than you think," he replies cryptically.

"There's a reason why we usually interrogate people before cutting out their tongues," I say pointedly. "I need a computer to do more digging about Bram's past. If I can find out more about him, it'll help."

"Go and speak to Penelope." Alaric nods. He won't suspect I want to check on something else. "She'll be able to help."

I nod curtly. Penelope encrypted our client database, so I will struggle to check our records myself, but Bram's supposed to be a computer genius. If he thinks Trout is a Killers Club member, he has to prove it.

I hop on the lift and ride to Penelope's office in the quietest dingy corner of HQ. I rarely come up here; I'm much happier punching bags. I get out and move through the room. It's filled with unused office chairs, tables, and printers; the only splash of colour is a cat tower in one corner. Penelope works in a private room off the main space.

I hover outside her door before knocking. Inside, the whirring of machines and mad typing on the keyboard signals she's home. Something clatters from inside, and an impatient voice calls, "Come in!"

I enter. Multiple screens are mounted around the walls. As soon as I step inside, she cuts them all to show screen-savers of her spoiled Siamese in different poses instead.

"Nice cat," I comment.

"Thanks," she says, stroking the furry demon curled in her lap. At one point, she had five cats, but Alaric set a one-cat limit when it looked like she was going to turn the floor into a rescue centre. "Her name is Pepper."

"Hi, Pepper," I coo, reaching to stroke her.

Pepper hisses, warning me that if my fingers touch her fur, she'll give me rabies. Fucking bitch.

"What can I do for you?" Penelope demands, shaking her messy bob in disapproval.

"Can't I just swing by to say hello to a friend?"

She crosses her arms. "You only come here when you want something."

It's a good thing she has Pepper for company. Unlike the rest of us, Penelope wasn't recruited because she was at death's door. Alaric staged her death because she was on the run from the FBI after she hacked into their system and sold secrets to the wrong people. If they catch her, they'll lock her up for life, or worse.

"I need a laptop," I say, eyeing up the case filled with them to my left. "For research."

"I can find it for you," she says, pushing her sliding glasses higher up her nose. "I'll be able to find anything you need much quicker."

Time for me to bullshit.

"It's not just a matter of finding information," I explain. "I'm doing an interrogation, and I want to show him pictures of certain places to really get into his head. I don't need to do anything sophisticated."

"Oh, you're talking about *him*." Her body language changes. Her shoulders tense, and she's hissing more than Pepper. "If you must."

"Is everything okay?" I ask. "You seem a little… on edge."

She spins around in her computer chair so quickly that she'll be lucky not to get whiplash. "Am I good at my job, Ivy?"

"The best," I reassure her. "You know you are."

"I thought so too," she says victoriously as if she's making a point and winning an argument in her head. Maybe I should speak to her more often. She wheels herself over to the stack of laptops and hands me one. "Here you go."

"Thanks," I reply, still confused by her outburst. Alaric needs to give her more credit. We can't lose someone like Penelope.

She turns her back on me, giving me my cue to leave.

"Thanks, Penelope."

"Bring it back when you're done," she snaps, then proceeds to take her pent-up anger out on the keyboard, smashing the keys and writing a string of code that makes zero sense to someone like me.

Maybe I'm mad for letting Bram's words get to me. I should trust Alaric, but creeping doubt tells me I'll regret it if I don't find out for myself.

# CHAPTER 27

## BRAM

vy's purposeful, heavy footsteps wake me from my broken sleep. She's on the warpath. I've been finding myself looking forward to her visits, but I shrink back against the wall now. The last time I saw her this mad, she stuck a branding iron in my chest. My nail beds have only started to heal over…

She opens the hatch and steps back against the wall so that I can see her from the middle up. My chest constricts. Her red hair is piled on top of her head in a messy bun with a few loose tendrils hanging out, letting me look at her face properly. Her full lips look so soft, and… nope. *Don't fucking go there.* She's beautiful, but she's fucking deadly.

She pulls a chair from further down the corridor and balances a backpack on it. She unzips it to pull out a laptop.

"I tried, but I couldn't find anything," she says in exasperation. Her eyes are ringed with black circles. She must have stayed awake all night looking for answers.

I shake my head. *Do you think they'd leave confidential client records lying around for anyone to find?*

This is a step forward, though. She listened to what I said and is questioning the Killers Club. Alaric was right to question her loyalty after all.

"You're supposed to be a computer guy," she says. "Tell me what to do."

How do I know this isn't Alaric testing me like he's testing Ivy? He could be double-crossing us both. But if he's not, this could work to my advantage. If she learns the true nature of the people she's working for, I could persuade her to set me free.

I make a swivel motion with my finger, signalling for her to turn the screen around. The opening is too small to pass the laptop through or for me to type. I look at the operating system and write exactly what sequence she needs to put in.

"None of this makes sense," she grumbles as she types in the code, then turns the screen around again for me to check. I give her a thumbs-up. "It's like speaking a whole robot language."

I write:

*This could take a while.*

"Do you have something better to do?" Her head snaps up. "It doesn't look like you're going anywhere to me."

I crack a smile.

*Let's get to work…*

Alaric never mentioned I couldn't help her hack into their system. If there's something here, I'll find it. The real question is, how will Ivy react when she finds out the secrets the Killers Club is hiding?

# CHAPTER 28

## SEB

can't believe it," I repeat for the hundredth time. We've been awake most of the night, talking through theories. I don't want to believe she works for the Killers Club, but everything points to it, and the sinking dread in my stomach tells me that Freddie's right.

I thought we knew her. The real her. She was the first woman who didn't care about my title or my family. A woman who saw the real me. How much of it was a lie? Did she know who I was when we first met? Have I been a pawn in her ruthless games? Was she using us the whole time?

"Her name is Ivy, remember?" Freddie spits. "And she *is* part of the Killers Club. We've been too stupid to see it."

Yesterday, Freddie was a shattered man. His heart fractured into a thousand pieces, but now a furious fire has ignited in his core.

"So, Spencer tried to kill her, but he didn't finish the job," I say, reviewing our suspected series of events. "Her story about witness protection was bullshit. The Killers Club found her—somehow—and they took her in. They trained her to be an assassin, and she's been working for them for the last five years."

"She once told me she worked overseas," Freddie says. "Maybe that's true."

"So they gave her a new identity," I continue. They've got the resources to make that happen. "Then she ran into me on a job when she was killing Danny. After that, Callen and Bram saw her having a drink with an agent. We thought we were protecting her, but she was a step ahead all along. Do you think she knew who we were from the start?"

"They know everything!" Freddie explodes, making me wince. Any softness he's shown since being reunited with Rose—Ivy—has been blasted away, replaced by a blood-thirsty resolve. "All she wanted was information. We meant nothing."

"Fuck!" I whirl around and punch the wall. I bet they've been laughing at our stupidity. "And what about Callen? That bastard had to know. Maybe he didn't trick her at all. She could have volunteered to take the bomb to the ball." I feel sick. "Look, I know we haven't talked about it since Callen left. I should have told you about the night when we—"

"I don't need to hear the sordid details," Freddie cuts me off. His icy glare sends a chill scurrying down my spine. "All that matters is finding Bram. We find her, we find the club, and we bring him home. That's our focus, but..." He grimaces like he's in physical pain. "We'll need help."

"Callen?" I scoff in disbelief. "Do you think he'll want to speak to us again after how we left things?"

"We have to try," Freddie says, walking to the window. We have a great view from our flat, and he surveys the hurrying figures on the street below. "Callen is already a step ahead if he knew about Rose. He won't be able to take on the Killers Club single-handedly. If we're going to save Bram, the three of us need to combine forces."

"He won't be interested unless we get on our knees and grovel," I say. "Even if we wanted to speak to him, how would we find him? He's probably in Scotland trying to pick a fight with the Loch Ness monster. You know what he was like before he joined us."

"I don't think we'll have any problem finding him." Freddie grins. "Now grab your coat. We're going for a walk."

"A walk?"

Maybe he's lost his mind. The revelation about Rose's real identity could have tipped him over the edge.

"Trust me," he says, already heading for the door. "Let's go."

# CHAPTER 29

## CALLEN

It was hard to get eyes on their building, but I managed it. I've watched them come and go over the last few days. I don't stay for long periods to avoid drawing any attention. I want to establish a pattern and understand their routine, which is challenging without directly passing by the house while switching vehicles and disguises.

Blondie and the tattooed boss are the only two people I've seen leaving the building. Their schedule isn't predictable; they leave and return at random times. I haven't found another entrance or exit in my search of the area, so they either have an underground tunnel stretching beneath the city or fewer agents in the building than I initially thought. Their organisation might not be as powerful as they made it out to be unless they have a secondary location. But my predatory instinct tells me I'm close.

Storming the building will take careful planning. Although I want to blow the door off its hinges, I need to wait until Blondie and her boyfriend are out to make my move. While waiting, I've spent time assembling an extra special explosion for the Killers Club. It was easy to get the supplies, and the hotel manager looked the other way when other guests complained about noises coming from my room.

I've been splitting my time between watching the Killers Club and keeping tabs on the Dukes. Freddie hasn't left the house in days like the sorry sack of shit he is. They keep the blinds permanently drawn, and I haven't been able to get a proper look inside. The fuckers are turning into vampires without me around. I don't know why I'm wasting my time watching them, but I can't help myself. It's a bad habit I'll need to shake, but not today…

I shuffle around on my motorbike seat. After an hour of watching the Killers Club's house in the rain, my arse is going numb, so I decide to loop back to the flats where the Dukes are staying before returning to the hotel.

I zig-zag through the London traffic and park up outside an office building opposite Freddie and Seb's hide-out—from my previous rounds of surveillance, I've learned that I can get the best view of their floor from inside it.

The foyer's empty when I enter. There's no reception desk or cameras—conveniently, they broke with some help from me, and they've not been fixed yet. I head to the waiting lift and jab the button to take me to the sixteenth floor.

I hum to myself to fill the silence until the lift pings. This is my stop. Luckily for me, the top floors have been recently vacated by a bankrupt company. I move through the corridor and let myself into the office. I picked the lock last week, and no one has come to check. Maintenance has their work cut out for them, between that and the cameras.

The office stretches around the entire floor; it's a graveyard of empty desks and chairs, but anything of real value has been seized by bailiffs. Behind limp blinds, a glass window spans across the entire sides of the building, which would turn it into a greenhouse in summer, and I head towards it to get the best view of the Dukes' flat.

Suddenly, there's a noise behind me.

What the… it sounded like a drawer opening and closing.

I whip my head around but only see old filing cabinets.

"Hello?" I call.

*Nothing.*

A swishing noise, like a coat sweeping close by, makes the hairs on my neck stand on end.

I'm not alone.

I draw my gun and hold it out in front of me. Three bullets are left, so I'll have to make them count. Failing that, I have a knife in my other pocket, and my knuckles are always my preferred first choice for a fight—the bloodier, the better.

I scan the area, but there's no sign of movement.

"Come on, don't be shy," I call. There's no answer. "Or do you want to play hide and seek?"

When I find them, I'll plant a bullet through their skull. I head to the nearest cabinet, slink down and press my back against it.

"Fuck!" My concentration slips as a fire alarm above my head blares out, almost bursting my eardrums. The deafening noise takes me by surprise and makes me stagger. My arm drops for a split second, and that's when they pounce.

A figure flies at me from out of nowhere. I see nothing but a black trench coat and a balaclava. They're slim build, shorter than me, and they're quick. Quick enough to plunge a needle into the side of my neck before I react.

Adrenaline kicks in. I thrash around like a shark caught in a fishing net. These few seconds count, and I fucking know it. I roar and arch my back, trying to throw them off before they can inject a full dose of whatever poison into me. I manage to knock them back, but the effects are already starting.

I have no energy to turn. The gun slips through my fingers as I stagger forward and reach for the desk to steady myself, but it's further away than it looks through my blurring vision. My coordination vanishes, and I collapse to my knees.

"You…you…" I stammer but can't get the words out.

A paralytic agent rushes through my bloodstream. I fight to keep myself upright but fall to the side. My head hits the scratchy grey carpeted floor, and I can do nothing to stop it.

In front of me, a lotus flower flutters delicately to the ground, and then everything goes black…

# CHAPTER 30

## IVY

"There!" I declare proudly, looking at Bram to give his final stamp of approval. "Ready?"

His eyebrows and nose are scrunched from concentrating hard, but he takes a deep breath and gives a curt nod.

It got rocky for a while with me using arrows that pointed in the wrong direction, but we made it. I've never coded before, and damn, I've grown a newfound appreciation for the work of developers over the last few hours. Bram tried to write the logic behind what we were doing, but I didn't understand it, so I told him to stick to writing what I needed to type. Nerds are fucking powerful.

"Here goes…" I murmur, hoping Bram hasn't lied and somehow allowed me to code in something that'll make the whole city explode like a supervillain.

I hit enter. There's no going back. A loading bar appears on the black screen with green text. Time slows to a crawl until the word 'Authorised' appears in a pop-up box with a ping.

"We did it!" I gasp.

Bram jumps and punches the air in victory, losing his composed exterior with what looks to be a genuine smile. His entire face transforms, smoothing out his harsh jawline and sharp cheekbones.

"So..." I look at the text on the screen. This is the first time I've seen the Killers Club client database. Alaric and Penelope are the only ones with access. Despite the exhilaration of hacking into the system, my palms are sweaty. Alaric would kill me if he found out what we'd done. "Are you sure Penelope won't be able to tell that we're snooping around?"

He grins smugly and shakes his head, almost laughing. *No way.* I've got to admire his confidence. His helping me only affirms he thinks there's something to find. He wouldn't risk it otherwise, right?

I hold up the laptop screen for him to see through the hatch. "What now?"

He rolls his eyes and points at the search bar at the top of the screen like I'm a total dummy.

"How am I meant to know it's the same as websites?" I mutter.

He clears his throat to catch my attention and writes a note:

*Put your search terms inside a ★*

"I'm not a complete idiot," I say, quickly adding in the stars before he sees I missed them.

I search for Christopher Trout.

*No results.*

"Nothing." I sigh. "See?

If he's sent me on a wild goose chase, I'll break into his

cell and strangle him.

Bram scribbles:

*Try Fishy.*

Bile rises in my throat just thinking about his nickname. Fishy is what Spencer used to call him. I swap out the search term, and my heart drops into my stomach when it returns one result.

With shaking fingers, I glide the cursor to the text and click it. When I do, a client profile appears. My stomach lurches—okay, I could *really* vomit this time seeing Christopher Trout's face staring back at me. The leering son of a bitch who raped and killed my sister deserves to die.

Bram knocks on the door, but I can't look away from the screen. I scroll, reading through his personal details and a list of all the jobs the Killers Club has completed for him. There are names on there I recognise. Names of marks I've killed. People I've killed for him!

Bram knocks again, louder this time.

"What?" I retort. His gaze softens as his eyes meet mine, making my skin crawl. "Don't look at me like that!"

He raises his eyebrows. *Like what?*

He can shove his pity right up his fucking arse. My entire life has been blown to smithereens with a simple search, just like the bomb that tore Lord McGowan apart limb from limb. There's no returning from this.

I thought Alaric was my saviour and looked up to him like a father figure. He reassured me that he had my best interests at heart and told me we were waiting until I had control of my anger to work through my hit list, but everything was a lie.

A name on the bottom of the job list makes my stomach churn. *Anthony Steel.* The date next to the job matches when Alaric said I could start working through my list. He never thought I was ready or that enough time had passed. No, it was always about the club. He knew I wanted to kill Anthony and used it to his advantage. If he's done this, what else is he capable of?

I've seen enough. I key in the command Bram taught me to shut everything down, then slam the laptop shut, resisting the urge to hurl it across the dungeon.

I've always known the Killers Club worked for bad people. Yet, I always saw us as helping to restore balance. I thought a minimum requirement for taking on a client would at least involve not killing an agent's family member.

Bram slides a note under the door.

*Are you okay?*

"Am I okay?" I take a deep breath to compose myself, but it doesn't help me from feeling like I've run a marathon. "What kind of question is that?" I hiss. "I've found out the club I've sworn my allegiance to is working for the man who killed my sister."

He tilts his head to the right. *What did you expect?*

"I knew they weren't perfect." I'm not naïve. We're assassins, not soup kitchen volunteers. But, whenever I killed someone, I knew it benefited others and the people I murdered weren't innocent either. "But to be working with him…" My bottom lip starts to tremble, and I sink my teeth into it to stop it. Bram can't see me like that. "Alaric knows what he did."

A war rages on inside my head. I want to scream! I want to tear this whole place down! I want to find Alaric and kill him myself! He's a liar and a manipulator. He's been using me—all of us—as his puppets for years. Bram was right; loyalty doesn't exist. The Killers Club doesn't care about us.

Bram watches me closely. *What are you going to do next?*

My knees go weak. I turn my back on him and slide down the door, sniffing to stop a tear from rolling down my cheek.

The truth is, I don't know. I really don't know.

# CHAPTER 31

## SEB

"Where are we going?" I ask, quickening my pace to keep up with Freddie's long strides. "This doesn't seem like the right time for a walk."

He ignores me and crosses the road to the high-rise offices. They're home to start-up companies. It's a depressing block but in an excellent location with reasonable rent, which makes it a great budget option. I expect us to keep walking, but Freddie stops and holds the door. "This way."

There's no reception desk, so we walk in without being questioned.

"Here?" I look around the empty, bleak foyer aside from a sad fake plant in the corner. "Why?"

"You'll see," Freddie replies, speeding across the foyer and slamming the lift button with his palm.

I scowl. "Don't you think we have enough mystery in our life?"

He grins. It's the first time I've seen my friend smile since the night of the Collingsbrook Ball. While it's nice to see him happy, I don't know what's coming when he's in a strange mood like this.

The lift doors open, and he steps in first. "Age before royalty."

"Fuck you," I mutter.

Once inside, Freddie's fingers hover over the buttons while selecting the floor, opting for the fifteenth. "That should be about right."

"You know we get the same view from our flat," I say sarcastically, crossing my arms and wrinkling my nose at the faint smell of piss. "What's up here?

"You'll see," Freddie replies cryptically.

As if we don't have enough mystery in our life with finding out the woman we fell for is a ruthless assassin.

"Fucking hell!" My hands fly to cover my ears to protect them from the sudden cry of a fire alarm.

Freddie's smile twists into a grimace as the lift halts on the tenth floor. "It looks like we're taking the stairs from here."

"Shouldn't we be leaving?" I ask, gesturing upward at the wailing siren.

"No." He frowns. "We need to hurry."

We rush to the nearest stairwell alongside other people spilling out of their offices. From their sense of urgency and hurried footsteps, this isn't a scheduled alarm.

We fight past the flood of bodies moving in the opposite direction. Some whisper my name as they pass us. After my recent publicity, it's hard to go anywhere without being recognised. I hate it—the whispers, the stares, the constant judgement, as if they know what it's like to live in my fucking shoes. I'll wear sunglasses the next time we venture out, even if it's raining. Maybe I'll even start wearing a mask like the men in the metal band Callen likes.

"Come on," Freddie yells. After peering into the fifteenth floor, Freddie waves his arm and points upwards. "It must be the next floor!"

"Are you—"

"Fucking move, Seb!" he barks, cutting me short of asking him whether he's having a mental breakdown.

There are no people coming down from above, so the upper floors appear to be deserted. We exit and burst onto the sixteenth floor.

Freddie leads the way through an open door into an abandoned office floor.

I frown, looking around. "There's nothing here."

We keep walking and turn a corner.

*No…*

A lifeless body lies on the floor. I'd recognise his long hair and signature leather jacket anywhere. A shadowy figure in a black trench coat looms over him like the Grim Reaper, holding a blade to his throat.

"Callen!" I yell.

His attacker turns to see us, caught off guard. A balaclava covers their face, leaving only a slit for their eyes. They jump into action at our interruption by fleeing in the opposite direction.

My legs are already moving. I sprint after them, slamming and pushing chairs out of the way. Freddie is close behind me. He takes out his gun and starts firing, but the figure dodges the bullets effortlessly. They're fast.

Before we get to Callen, the figure is already out another door on the far side of the floor.

"Go!" Freddie roars. I'm a better runner.

I'm a few seconds behind Callen's attacker and run

through the exit into an eerily empty foyer. The lifts are out of service because of the alarm, and there are two separate staircases. Which do I choose?

I make a split-second decision and pick the one on the right. When I peer down, office workers are still making their way outside. I race to the other one. There's no sign of the attacker, but concerned cries float up from below.

"Was that a gun?"

"Did you hear that?"

The figure could be on any floor in the building by now. I won't be able to find them by myself. There's too much ground to cover, and I can't be associated with another public scandal.

I kick the door to take out my frustration, and it bounces off the wall with a bang to mask my frustrated yell, "Fuck!"

I turn, abandoning the chase to return to Callen's side.

Right now, he's the priority. We've let him down once before. We won't do it again. Freddie kneels at Callen's side, holding his wrist to check his pulse. Callen's eyes are closed.

"They got away," I stammer. "I tried—"

"It's a setback, but we'll find them," Freddie cuts me off.

"Is he…"

"He's still alive," Freddie confirms.

"Thank fuck for that." I breathe a sigh of relief, then notice the cut on Callen's neck. It's the start of an incision right on his artery. If we arrived a split second later, we'd be finding Callen's head spinning on a swivel chair. "It looks like we got here in time."

"He's survived worse," Freddie says gruffly.

"How did you know he was here?"

"He's been watching us for days," Freddie says. "Callen may be the biggest pain in our arses, but he is one of us—whether we, or he, likes it or not. He's always going to find his way back."

I shake my head in disbelief. "The sneaky son of a bitch."

I'll have to think of stalker jokes to tease him about when he comes around. If Callen's made an enemy out of someone, we can't have him unguarded in the hospital. He's coming with us.

Freddie nods. "Callen was watching us, but someone else was watching him."

"Trust Callen to make another enemy," I say. Something pink catches my eye under a nearby table. I bend to pick up a lotus flower and turn it in my hands. "Someone who likes flowers."

"This has the Killers Club written all over it," Freddie says. "Do you remember what they found with Doyle's body?"

On the nearest desk, something else catches my eye. "It's not just the flower…"

A note is propped up:

*With love, the K.C. x*

We need to get him out of here and move to another location," Freddie says. "If someone followed Callen, they must have known he was watching us, too."

We're not safe anywhere now that a group of assassins has us in their sights.

# CHAPTER 32

## BRAM

She tries to steady her shaky breathing to hide her feelings from me, but it doesn't work. A few inches away, on the other side of that door, her entire world is falling apart.

*You weren't to know.*

"But why him?" Her voice is desperate, confused, and broken. I'm not speaking to the brutal Killers Club agent. I'm talking to the real Ivy Penrose. "Alaric knows what he did. Why would he work with him?"

Because they're monsters, I answer in my head. He lives for spilling blood and having power. Alaric acted the same way in the army, and he hasn't changed. He's manipulating everyone.

"I should have known," she stammers. "How didn't I know? I have to speak to him!" She jumps up. "I have to see what he has to say. I—"

I pound my fists on the door, enough to make her stop.

Her glistening eyes peer through the window and pierce through my skin.

One look at my face dulls her enthusiasm.

I shake my head. *He'll kill you.*

She swallows as the realisation dawns on her. I'm right. He'd slit her pretty little throat without hesitation. There are plenty of people with vendettas he can groom to take her place.

Alaric pretends to give second chances, but he exploits people instead. That's why I'll never trust him, no matter what I've agreed to.

"How am I meant to keep on pretending?" Ivy asks. "What am I meant to do now? I don't exist. There's no record of me anywhere. It's not like I can leave!"

*The Dukes.*

"I've been lying to them." She hangs her head. "I'm no better than Alaric."

I feel her pain, but I have to push that aside. As a soldier, they taught me to switch off my emotions, and I do that now. Her heart is cracking open, but she's my ticket to freedom. My eyes stray to the door handle. This is the moment I've waited for. A moment of weakness.

The pen is moving across the paper before I have second thoughts.

*I could help you build a new identity.*
*I know the code to the door.*

"You want me to let you out?"

Guilt claws at my skin as I nod slowly and write the numbers down.

6, 8, 2, 1.

"I can't," she says. "He'll find out. They'll know it was me. I…"

I hold up a note before she has any more time to think about it. I'm getting to her. I can feel it…

*What have you got left to lose? I'm the only one who can help.*

"You're right." A sad smile makes her lips twitch. "I've got nothing to lose."

Her fingers shake as she presses the number six and then reaches for the next number.

I grunt, making her stop before she presses the second number. I thought I could, but I can't… even after what she's done. She's as broken as I am. If I make her do this, I'm signing her death warrant.

"What?" Ivy pauses. "I thought this is what you wanted?"

But it's already too late.

Crashing footsteps grow closer. Her wide, beautiful eyes blink up at me, narrowing in confusion, and I step back, unable to meet her watchful gaze. I had her. For that split second, she trusted me… and I took advantage.

"Bram…" she whispers, her sentence trailing off as the blood drains from my face. "What did you do?"

There's no time to grab a pen to explain.

Her head whips around to see Alaric standing at the end of the corridor.

"Ivy," Alaric's chilling voice booms. "You've failed my test."

"Test?" She tries to hold her nerve, but her voice trembles slightly. If I've noticed, Alaric will have too. "What do you mean?"

"It's against our rules to release a prisoner," he sneers.

"I…" Her voice falters, fading into nothing. "I didn't… I didn't mean…"

"You failed." His indifferent tone sends chills down my spine. His moods change like the flick of a switch, going from being your friend one minute to an enemy the next. "You're ineffective."

Ivy composes herself, throws her shoulders back and draws herself up to full height—even though she's no match for him, she won't go down without a fight.

"You lied to me," she hisses in accusation. "Christopher Trout is one of our clients!"

Alaric's steps echo. He regards the laptop at Ivy's feet, then appears next to the cell to goad me through the opening. "It looks like you've failed your test too, Bram."

*Eat shit, motherfucker.*

"Do you think we'd ever mention a client's name in front of a prisoner?" Alaric tuts, wagging his finger at me. "I wanted to see whether you were paying attention. I have to give you credit for being observant, but how can I trust someone who leaks information to the enemy? Considering your talents, it's a shame you won't ever be a Killers Club agent."

Ivy charges at him. "You're a monster!"

"Look around, Ivy," Alaric replies, unfazed as her fists bounce off his muscular chest without budging an inch.

He catches her wrists. "We're all monsters here. That's what makes us a family."

"I want out," she sneers. "I don't want to be part of this anymore. I don't want to be in the Killers Club."

"Out?" Alaric laughs, letting Ivy's arms fall to her sides. "There is no out for someone like you. You're in, or you're dead."

"What're you going to do?" she challenges, raising an eyebrow. "Kill me?"

"Oh no, I have a better idea…"

Distant heels click on the stone floor, growing closer.

"Steph!" Ivy sounds almost relieved to see her. That's a mistake. "You have to help me."

"You let us down, Ive," Stephanie replies like a brainwashed cult follower. "We don't have a choice."

"I thought we were friends," Ivy says, stepping back.

*No!* I want to scream. *Don't lose your fight now!* But she's losing any hope, becoming resigned to her imminent death.

"We didn't want it to come to this," the blonde bitch replies. "But the club comes above all else."

Someone clicks the safety off their gun, and Alaric snaps the cell window shut so I can't see what's happening. I kick the door. It won't stop them from blowing her brains out, but at least she'll know someone cared whether she lived or died.

I imagine them pointing the barrel at her, expecting it to fire any second, but it doesn't…

The hinges to my cell creak.

"Step away from the door, pretty boy," Stephanie threatens, appearing in the doorway, "or I'll redecorate this cell."

Next to her, Alaric's fingers dig into Ivy's arms so hard

that her skin bulges in his grasp. He presses his gun into her forehead while Stephanie aims hers at me. Ivy tries to shrug Alaric off and says, "If you're going to kill me, fucking do it."

"I have a better idea," Alaric says, grinning. "I want to give you both a final chance at redemption and more time to think about what you've done."

He throws Ivy in my direction, and she goes flying from the force. I run to catch her, but Stephanie is quick on the trigger. She fires a shot to punish me for moving. It skims my thigh and slices through the skin but misses my major artery. I stagger as Ivy breaks her fall with her hands.

"The last one alive gets a free pass," Alaric says, slamming the door shut behind us.

Ivy's panting, and I offer my hand to help her to her feet. In response, her head snaps up, and her venomous glare is enough to make me hold up my hands and back away.

# CHAPTER 33

IVY

Alaric and Stephanie leave silence and destruction in their wake. They have split my world in two. Everything I knew about my life with the Killers Club was bullshit, and my body shakes from the shock.

Bram—the traitor!—offers me his hand, then changes his mind. Good fucking riddance! He's lucky I'm in shock, otherwise, he'd have a broken wrist. I haul myself upwards without Bram's help.

"Stephanie!" I go to the door and pummel my fists against it. "Alaric! This isn't funny!"

I keep banging, but there's no response…

I don't want to turn around and face Bram yet. I can't. Doing that will mean accepting that the people I've known for years never truly cared about me. If they can shut me out so quickly, I'm nothing more than a loaded gun and another weapon on their shelf.

"Come on!" My voice grows hoarse as the minutes pass, but I push aside the scratchy feeling at the back of my throat. "Let me out!"

No one returns to tell me this was a joke. Nope, this is

happening. I'm not a Killers Club agent anymore, I'm their prisoner.

Out of the corner of my eye, a blood trail on the concrete floor catches my attention. I spin slowly to find Bram cradling his leg on the floor. He's shirtless and uses his teeth to rip what's left of his t-shirt into strips. He winces in pain as he wraps them around the wound with his bloodstained hands. The offending bullet lies a few feet away.

He catches me staring and arches an eyebrow as if to ask whether I will help.

"It's just a scratch," I bark, refusing to kneel. "It's a shame it didn't go through your head."

Maybe I should kill him now. It'd be easy to snap his neck when he's in this position. A quick twist of my wrist would put him out of his misery. He's vulnerable, and seeing his shredded muscles in their full glory makes me aware this might be my last chance at an advantage.

*You need to think, Ivy.* Don't give in to the rising panic. If you do, it'll wash over you like waves and drown you. I need to be strong.

Bram scowls and secures the fabric in place with a tight knot. He shuffles to the opposite corner of the cell, as far away from me as possible in the small space. The moody prick crosses his arms over his hairy chest, making his biceps bulge, and has the cheek to glower at me.

"I don't have time to kiss your boo-boos better," I retort. "Can't you see we're in a bad situation here?"

He rolls his eyes. *Welcome to the fucking club.*

"Don't look at me like that." I jab my finger accusingly in his direction. "It's your fault I'm here. You were trying to set me up!"

Would I have done the same in this position? I skim my

fingers around the edges of the door holding us hostage, but it's useless. We specially designed the cells to be escape-proof.

Bram wipes his hands with the remnants of his t-shirt, then writes a message and holds it up to show me.

*I won't kill you.*

Is that supposed to make me feel better? I snatch the note from his hands, not caring whether I give him a paper cut. I screw it into a ball and imagine it's his face I'm crushing, then throw it at his head. It bounces off his forehead, and his eyes widen in outrage as he watches the ball rebound and roll across the floor.

"That's brilliant. Do you want me to thank you for being such a fucking gentleman?" I scoff. "You're worse than Seb."

His eyes light up at the mention of his friend's name, even in this context.

"If you kill me, you get to see Seb again," I remind him. "Doesn't that make you want to do it?" He stares back blankly. "You're impossible!"

He writes:

*Kill me. It's what you want. Do it.*

"It's no fun if you want me to kill you!" I huff in exasperation. "That's like admitting you've won."

He shakes his head. *I can't win.*

My blood simmers with a building fury, making my head want to explode. I can't stand it. I can't…

And I scream.

Bram's hands fly to his ears while I let loose. I scream until my lungs burn and my eardrums ring. I don't stop. I let all my emotions flood into the air: the bitter betrayal, the heart-wrenching hurt, the fake relationships, and the fucking lies!

My chest heaves. I stop to gasp for air and realise a figure is standing behind me. The warmth from Bram's body radiates against mine.

I turn, almost walking into his pecs and disjointing my nose. I'm a curvy girl, but the shadow of his giant silhouette swallows me whole.

"What're you going to do?" I pant. "Kill me?"

The owl on his throat tattoo stares back in silent judgement.

"Go on!" I slam my fists into his chest. "Do it!"

He doesn't budge. I punch him repeatedly, taking out all my frustration, like he's a punching bag. It's draining my energy, each punch getting weaker than the last. I know I should stop to conserve my strength—maybe this is part of Bram's grand plan—but I don't.

Uncontrollable tears roll down my cheeks as I keep pummelling him.

"Fight back!" I scream at the human wall. "Fucking fight back like a man!"

Bram doesn't react. My words deflect off his muscles like my punches.

"React!" I yell. "Why aren't—"

Suddenly, his giant hands catch my fists in his grasp. Our eyes meet, sharing in our pain and suffering. I feel something else…

Safety. I'm pulled into a ghost of a memory. A reassuring voice. A car journey. Someone was watching out for me.

His toasty palms cradle my hands firmly. If he's mad about my outburst, he doesn't show it. We don't move, and I catch my breath while he stands motionless like a statue.

Finally, I yank myself out of his hypnotic trance. The side of Bram's mouth twitches up in a half-grin, and he leans against the wall to watch me.

His eyes sparkle and ask: *What's your next move?*

"I'm getting out of here," I say.

Well, I was going to try…

# CHAPTER 34

## BRAM

She's a tornado of emotions in a confined space. Her emotions circle like a vortex, sucking everything inside it, including me. She consumes me, and I embody her pain as if it's my own, making me want to do anything to make the weight of it stop.

I feel her eruption of anger, the crushing sadness, and, worst of all, the emptiness left behind.

She paces like a prowling animal. My chest stings from her punches, but it's what I deserve. Even though I had second thoughts and tried to stop her, it was too late. As soon as she hit that first button, Alaric was on his way.

I should have known better than to follow Alaric's orders. Haven't I learned from the past that he will say anything to get what he wants? Now, I'm locked in a space with a pocket rocket ready to launch.

"They wouldn't do this," she murmurs, shaking her head. She's incoherent, saying long trailing sentences under her breath that don't make sense. "This can't be happening. They wouldn't… I don't…"

I sit down as she thumps on the door again. It's pointless, and she'll tire soon enough.

"Let me out!" Ivy yells. "Alaric! Stephanie!"

They won't answer her calls. Not yet, anyway. If they left her with me, they had to be willing to let her die. For all they knew, I could have wrapped my hands around her throat the moment they threw her inside.

I doodle to distract myself from the shooting pain in my leg. The bullet went deeper than I thought. Stephanie's an excellent shot.

I prefer working with paint. I like how oils glide and mix over a canvas, but the scratchy Biro on cheap paper matches our circumstances. I draw nothing in particular, swirling shapes that ground me. Art keeps me sane and helps me think straight.

I remember when Freddie told me I could buy art for the Dukes' base. He and the others don't understand art or see its importance, but I do. It helps you make sense of things. It makes you *feel*.

Instead of going to expensive galleries, I prefer buying art from those who sell it at markets for less than the price of a bottle of wine. I spent time on the streets, searching for the next Picasso, seeking potential. I sense the artist's emotions behind their brush strokes. Abstract art isn't a case of spraying colours to see what works together, contrary to what most people think. It's purposeful. It has meaning. That's when I started making art of my own.

After a while, I started selling it on the down low—not that I wanted any credit. It's not about the money for me, it's about the process, which is why I protect my anonymity. The Dukes' base houses my personal collection. They know the paintings are by a mysterious artist called Raptor, but they don't know he's my alter ego…

While Ivy keeps shouting, drawing allows me to

drown her out. Eventually, her voice turns gravelly. When she finally gives up, she turns her attention to me.

"You're drawing?" Her jaw drops in disbelief. "Now?"

What else do I have to do? My entertainment options are limited, and I've already decided that I'm not playing the Killers Club's sick game. I won't kill her; I've already got too much blood on my hands.

"What's wrong with you?" she demands. "Why aren't you doing something? One of us has to die!"

I shrug. I made peace with my death the moment they took me. Death doesn't scare me. Living is scarier. It's a miracle my heart is still beating at all.

"You've given up." She snatches the paper from me and tears it in half, ruining my sketch. I won't kill her, but she still makes me fucking angry. "Aren't you at least going to try?"

I rise to my feet, and my nostrils flare as I stare at the ripped paper. *You shouldn't have done that.*

"Aren't you mad?" She pushes for a reaction. Her face shines with sweat from banging on the door so hard that her knuckles have minor cuts over the bone. "Don't you want to get out of here? You know what you have to do!"

She has a fucking death wish, and my inaction only infuriates her. She's like Callen. If he were here, he'd give her the fight she wants, but I won't give in.

"Do it!" she screams. Her voice cracks for a second. "Don't just stand there staring at me with that look on your face."

*What look?*

"You're fucking impossible!"

We don't need to use words to communicate anymore. She understands what I'm saying through my expressions alone, which is rare. It took the Dukes a while to speak my language. Seb picked it up quicker than the others, but it's different with Ivy. She sees straight into my mind.

*I don't know what you want from me.*

She wails in exasperation, then grabs my hands. They're still streaked with my blood. I've stemmed the flow for the time being, but if I don't get medical attention, it'll likely get infected, and it'll kill me if a psycho redhead doesn't kill me first.

She guides my hands to her throat, unravels my fingers and places them around her neck.

"See?" she taunts. She doesn't back down easily. "It's not that hard. All you have to do is squeeze."

*Is this what you want?*

She lets go. Her pulse jumps under my grip as I'm left holding her unassisted. Why is she pushing me to be the person I left behind? She knows what she's doing. This is a form of torture.

"See?" she encourages. "That's all you have to do, Bram."

*I won't.* My arms flop to my sides like limp pieces of lettuce. *I'm not going to hurt you.*

"I thought you were a killer!" Most people would be glad they're not getting choked to death, but she's acting like I've committed an unforgivable crime. "Alaric said you had no control and didn't know your strength. He told me you used to kill anything in sight—man, woman, and child! Where's that man? Where is he?"

Her words strike a match inside me. This time, I don't need her encouragement. Her eyes widen as I grab her by the throat and slam her backwards into the wall.

*Is this what you want, Ivy?* I'm not using my full strength. *Is this the man you want me to be?*

Her lips part as her breathing comes in violent,

wheezing bursts. My gaze lingers on them for a little too long. I squeeze tighter, making her cheeks flush a rosy pink. Killing her wouldn't take long. I narrow my eyes and watch her reaction.

"See?" she gasps. A victorious, twisted smile lights up her face. "I knew you could do it."

*You're unbelievable.*

I should hate her. This crazy bitch tortured me and put me through hell, but all I see squirming in my hand is a woman who needs help. A woman who needs a second chance, just like Freddie gave me.

I step closer, making her tits press against my chest. I can't stop myself from wondering how she tastes and how good her skin feels. Maybe I am more of a monster than I thought…

I lean in, my face within touching distance of hers. Her pupils dilate. *I'm not going to kill you.* Her breath heats my cheeks as my lips brush against hers, teasing her. I hesitate, expecting her to push me away, but she doesn't. We both know the Killers Club won't stop until one of us dies. After that, they'll kill whoever is left standing.

Our gaze meets, each of us staring in a standoff as I feel her pulse quicken. I hate her, but I want to have her. She's the first woman in a long time that's stirred my desire. I lean in again, my lips grazing gently over hers while she stays frozen in place, not daring to breathe. I pull back, studying her again, asking her a silent question. *What do we have to lose?*

I kiss her again, and she responds this time. Her tongue flicks out, licking along the opening of my lips, but I keep them closed. That's a line we don't cross. I squeeze her throat in warning and growl. *Don't push me.*

Something inside her snaps, like her defensive instincts

suddenly kick in, and she launches at me like a wild animal, clawing at my back with her nails for me to let go. Her scratches sting, but it doesn't dampen the lust coursing through my body like wildfire. I release my hold, and while she gasps for air, I move my hands to her face, cradling it.

I stare at her intently. *Do you want this?*

She shakes her head. She's a killer, but she's broken. Broken like me. I may have let her go, but I don't want to stop what we've started.

I reach for her t-shirt and tug it over her head, revealing her round tits spilling from her black bra. I've not slept with a woman for years, not since before the army. My cock is the hardest it's ever been. She's toxic but irresistible.

"We should be trying to kill each other," she moans as my lips move to her neck, trailing down it.

I grunt as I look into her eyes to answer. *We should, but isn't this better?*

I unclip her bra, and it falls to the floor. *Fuck.* Her nipples are gorgeous, almost heart-shaped. I run my hand down her stomach and push her legs apart. I meet her determined brown-eyed gaze as I slide my hand into her knickers. I immediately think she'll twist my arm behind my back and use this as a ruse to kill me. Except she doesn't.

I feel like we're playing a game. Seeing how far we can push the other one. I continue over her smooth mound, daring her to stop me. She doesn't, yet. My fingers slide along her hot, slippery slit.

"Bram," she groans as I probe between her lips, circling her wetness.

I move to her clit, making her whine in my ear. I tease,

alternating the pressure and strokes before slipping a finger inside her, then two. Her breathing grows feverish, thrusting her pussy into my palm as her inner thighs quake. Maybe she'll let me make her come before she kills me.

I use my other hand to force her to look up at me. A command hides behind my stare. *Spread your legs wider.* She flutters her eyelashes. *Let me explore your wet pussy and fucking enjoy it.*

God, I need her. I pull out my glistening-tipped fingers to tug down her skirt and knickers. She steps out of them in a hurry.

A bead of pre-cum slips from my tip at her naked body standing before me. Her smooth freckled skin has scars, no doubt from the accident, but she's strong. She's curvy but has firm muscles from years of training and deliciously thick thighs that I want to bury my face between.

She sinks to her knees, throwing her red hair over her shoulder. Her tresses trail down her back, resting above her arse as she runs her hands up my thighs. She pauses at the crudely wrapped blood-stained strips of fabric wrapped around my wound and asks, "Are you…"

I nod, clearing my throat. Her hands keep going, kneading my inner thighs. I swallow hard as her hand glides over the top of my trousers, letting her feel how hard she makes me. I'm worried I'll come from her touch alone, but I regain control, rubbing my fingers together to remind myself of how wet she is and how much she needs me.

She tugs my trousers off and unleashes my cock with urgency. This could be the last fuck either of us ever has. Her hot breath warms the tip of my cock. My eyes roll back in my head as she takes my shaft in her fist and guides it into her open mouth. She shouldn't have this effect on me, but I can't help it. Her pointed tongue licks my throbbing veins like I'm a fucking cornetto while maintaining eye contact.

*Can you see how hard you make me?*

I weave my fingers through her hair as her lips make a suction seal around me, making my whole body vibrate with longing. Her teasing is over, and she's not gentle. She opens wide and pushes me down her throat, gagging to fit as much of me in as she can. She makes slurping noises, and spit drips down her chin. The sound of it hitting the floor echoes like the drop of a pin.

Her tongue wriggling against me makes my hips jolt, and I thrust deeper down her throat. Hell, if I'm not careful, I'll choke her to death without using my hands. Primal desire has taken over, overruling my other judgements. Now I see why Seb was hypnotised by her.

I grab a fistful of her hair and yank her off.

"What's wrong?" she asks, wiping her mouth with a smirk. "I thought you were enjoying yourself."

*Get up.* I tug her hair and don't let go, pulling her to her feet. She stands to face me. This isn't a fancy hotel or limousine, but she takes my negative thoughts away even in a locked cell, facing imminent death.

I squeeze her arse, kneading her flesh, then lift her into the air. She wraps her legs around me tightly, trapping me with her thighs. She moans while my cock rubs against her wet entrance, sliding behind her lips but not inside. Not yet. I have to be sure…

"Just fuck me already!" she gasps. "What are you wai—"

Her words turn into a long moan, and her eyes flutter closed as I enter her to shut her up.

# CHAPTER 35

## IVY

"Yes!" I cry as Bram's cock slides deeper inside me. God, he feels good—too fucking good! Alaric locked us in here for a cage-fighting match to the death. Instead, it's devolved into a fuck fest. "Oh fuck, yes!"

His powerful arms hold my weight effortlessly, anchoring me in position—not just on his massive joystick but to the world. Right now, we are each other's entire universe. We're all we've got to hang onto. He won't drop me. That would admit defeat. We're not just fucking because we might die. We're fucking to live.

He grips my arse, lowering my pussy onto him. I sigh, focusing on nothing except each throbbing inch, and his rock-hard muscles push against me. I breathe in his scent —an irresistible, earthy tone that reminds me of a forest during a storm with a hint of blood like we're on the battlefield.

He backs away until the cold door presses against my spine. A door that seals us from everything outside it. The only barrier stopping us from escaping. A door that I now hope stays shut for a little longer…

I run my fingers through his hair, drawing his face to mine. We don't kiss, but our mouths are almost touching. His panting tickles my lips.

I clench my thighs around his torso, and my pussy tightens to hold him prisoner.

"You should have killed me," I murmur as he guides my pussy purposefully up and down his shaft. Each stroke rubs my clamping inner walls, teasing drops of pleasure from me I didn't even know existed. "Fuck, Bram… Don't stop."

All my sensations are heightened. Maybe it's because we shouldn't be doing this. Maybe it's because my whole life has been blown apart, or maybe it's because this could be the last day of our lives. Whatever the reason, the pleasure is all-consuming and so intense that it rolls through me, making me tremble.

My pussy squeezes him tightly, and I cry out like a wildcat. I need this. I need to be filled by this giant mountain of a man, and from the glint of lust in his eyes, he needs it too. We were on opposite sides, but now we're together.

We fall into a pattern, like a high tide crashing into rocks. I claw and scratch, clinging on and fighting for release. It spurs him on more. He pounds harder, using my body to make sure that he's all I'm thinking about… and how he's making me his.

"Yes!" I buck my hips, and the angle hits my clit to match his thrusts.

He eyes my bouncing tits hungrily and grunts, slowly edging himself out until his cock almost falls out of my pussy.

"Br—"

Before I get my words out, he slams me down again, forcing me to swallow him whole. My pussy aches. His cock matches his appearance—long and girthy.

My eyelids flutter shut, embracing the moment. A sheen of sweat and smeared blood covers our naked skin.

My legs quiver. I sink my teeth into his shoulder to contain my screams while he bucks faster. He's an uncontrollable force.

Although he can't talk, I sense how he's feeling. His eyes seem to change colour with his moods, and the minute changes to his expression let me know what he's thinking. He's different when he fucks. Usually, he's calm and composed, but now? He's a fucking animal.

I whimper as he rails into me. I want more. I want this. I need him to take it all away. My toes curl.

"I'm…"

My sentence trails off as I lose the ability to speak and scream as he draws an orgasm out of me. My insides clench so tightly that I'm worried I'll pass out, and I gush over his shaft. His grip on my arse tightens, holding hard enough that I'll bruise.

I lose track of time. My orgasm seems endless, peak after peak. Bram doesn't stop, refusing to let any wetness spill out of me.

His eyes meet mine, and I order, "Come for me, Bram."

He thrusts and grunts, spilling himself inside me.

For a few seconds, we stand there, frozen in time, breathless and spent. Then, I remember where we are and why we're here.

"Put me down," I order, extinguishing the moment.

*Fuck, what have I done?*

# CHAPTER 36

BRAM

She hurriedly puts on her t-shirt, and I grab the water bottle for her to clean herself. My cum seeps out of her pussy, decorating her inner thighs, but she shakes her head.

*But I want to make sure you're comfortable.*

"We're not wasting the last of our water on that," Ivy says. She slides a finger along the white liquid trailing out of her, then pops it into her mouth to lick it clean. She notices my eyes widen and scowls. "I've got to stay hydrated somehow, right?"

She turns away, unable to look in my direction, and puts the rest of her clothes back on. I do the same. The moment has passed. She rakes a hand through her red hair, trying to yank out any knots and tangles.

"We shouldn't have done that," she mumbles. "It was a bad idea."

When I look at her, I don't see a killer anymore. She's someone I have to protect. My survival instinct kicks in stronger than it has since I've been here. I thought I deserved to be kidnapped by the Killers Club as a punishment for everything I've done, but Ivy doesn't deserve to die like this. She won't die on my watch.

Saving her is my reason to keep going, and fucking her has reminded me of what I have to live for. Despite Alaric's attempts to change my allegiance, I'll never be one of his Killers Club agents. I'm a Duke. I may not want to protect myself, but I joined them to protect people. That's what we do.

I grab her shoulders and spin her around. She doesn't wrestle from my grip as I put my finger under her chin and move her face to look at me. *We're going to get out of here.*

"You don't know them like I do," she whispers. "We're going to die here."

*No, you can't give up.* I shake my head. *I refuse to let you.*

"They will stop at nothing to get what they want." She leans against the wall, then slides down it, pulling her knees to her chest to hug them. "We're going to die here, and if you don't kill me, we'll slowly starve to death."

During my time serving overseas, I fought against enemy soldiers, avoided bomb blasts, jumped over landmines, and looked down the barrels of countless guns. I refuse to starve to death. I saved her once, and I'll do it again.

I sit on the floor. She watches on curiously as I draw. This time, I add embellishments: stripes, stars, hearts… the works. When I'm done, I hold my masterpiece up to inspect it. Perfect. I grin, then slide it across to Ivy.

"Another cock and balls? With piercings and tattoos?" A smile plays on her lips, making my heart do a backflip, and then she laughs. She laughs so hard that her shoulders shake, and I join in.

I cautiously shuffle over next to her.

"You know, you could have added a Jacob's ladder," she teases.

I hand her a pen. *Go right ahead.*

She giggles as we add details to the penis, making it shoot dinosaur-shaped globs of cum and giving it Mickey Mouse ears. Ivy can't draw to save her life, but she's having fun, and it's taking her mind off our situation. That's what we used to do in the army—sat around making jokes, kept ourselves busy, and maintained high spirits, no matter what happened outside our tent.

"You need to put this one in a pretty gold frame." She laughs and puts the final touch on it. "It can go with the rest of your collection in the Dukes' base."

I tense and write.

*You've seen the paintings?*

"How could I miss them?" she says. "They're beautiful, but something was haunting about them too. Freddie told me you knew the artist."

My chest constricts. Do I take my secret to the grave?

I gulp and reply.

*They're my paintings.*
*I'm Raptor.*

"And you didn't tell the Dukes?"

I shake my head.

"Well, I guess I wasn't the only one keeping secrets from them." She smiles wistfully as I fold our drawing and tuck it into my pocket. If we do get out of here, the dick portrait can go right above our mantlepiece. "They miss you."

Her smile dulls. I act without thinking and put my arm around her shoulders. She inhales sharply, readying to punch me. I worry I've gone too far, but she changes her mind and leans into my chest, nuzzling my muscles like a kitten.

I hold her, feeling her beating heart through my clothes. With my spare hand, I write a note.

*We're in this together.*

She takes a deep breath and holds out her pinkie finger.

*Pinkie promise?*

I latch my finger around hers and squeeze.

*Pinkie promise.*

Ivy doesn't know it, but she's given me a reason to live.

# CHAPTER 37

## CALLEN

Holy steaming shit with a cherry on top…

I wake in unfamiliar surroundings. My head hasn't felt like this since Burns Night in Edinburgh at the turning of the millennium.

A familiar voice chirps, "Good morning, sleepyhead."

I roll over and groan at Seb's smug grin. The bastard's enjoying this too much.

"I always knew you were obsessed with me," I mutter. My mouth is drier than a bagpiper's. "If I'm not dead, kill me now."

"I brought you a cup of tea," he says, then yells loudly with the enthusiasm of a Golden Retriever puppy, "He's awake!"

"Keep it down," I growl, pulling myself up into a seated position in the bed. I'm tempted to throw the tea over Seb to wipe away his smirk, but I need my hit.

"Looks like there's no permanent damage," Seb comments.

The last thing I remember is stalking through an abandoned office like Bruce Willis in Die Hard, then... a fluttering lotus flower.

"Where am I?" I ask, looking around. They've put me on a sofa I'm too tall for, and my legs hang over the edge. Seb reaches out for my tea, but I snap, "I can get it myself."

The sugary liquid is lukewarm and under-brewed, but it'll have to do. How a lad with royal blood can make such a shite cuppa is beyond me. The only decent thing the English have ever done, beyond fish and chips, is brew tea.

Freddie appears in the room, leaning against the doorway. He's wearing an impeccable suit, and he's freshly shaven.

"We're at another one of our properties," Freddie answers, then raises his eyebrows. "One you didn't know about."

I hear the accusation in his tone and slurp my tea loudly. "You knew I was watching you. So what?"

"It looks like someone was following you, too," Freddie counters.

"Bastard," I mutter, covering my bruised ego.

"What happened?" Seb asks. "Did you get a look at who it was?"

"They snuck up on me from behind," I say, clutching the mug handle so tightly that it shakes. "You should have left me there. I'm not a Duke, remember? You made that clear."

My eyes focus now that I have some of Yorkshire's finest in my bloodstream. Behind Seb, photographs are pinned to a corkboard on the wall. There are images of Rose, Spencer, other faces I don't recognise, and different locations.

What do they know?

I nod at their collage that would put a stalker to shame.

"What are you working on?" I smirk. "Have you found out Rose isn't so fucking perfect after all?"

"What do you know?" Seb demands.

"Why should I tell you anything about your precious princess?" I laugh coldly. "You threw me out."

Freddie grimaces and swallows hard like he's chugging down shards of glass. He takes a deep breath. "We…"

"Go on." I narrow my eyes, putting the tea on the coffee table nearby. Freddie's gaze hardens when I don't put it on the coaster. He's a neat freak. "Say it. You were wrong."

"See?" Seb throws his arms in the air. "Didn't I tell you he'd be like this?"

I tap an invisible watch on my wrist. "I'm waiting."

"We… I… was wrong," Freddie says. It'll pain Mr Self-Fucking-Righteous to admit a mistake. "I… I let my emotions cloud my judgement. You were right."

"Say it again." His words are music to my ears. "Tell me how right I was."

"Don't push it," Freddie warns. "We saved your life, remember? We could take it just as easily."

"So we're even," I declare. "Why should I tell you anything?"

"Because you're a Duke," Seb says. "You wouldn't have kept watching us if you didn't care."

I shrug nonchalantly, refusing to admit that he's right. "I had a lot of free time on my hands."

"Cut the bullshit," Freddie barks. "We know you, and we know you were right about Rose. She's not who she says she is."

I clap my hands slowly, and Freddie's cheeks flush.

"Do you want a medal for finally working that out?" I taunt. "Is it the lack of pussy that made you finally see it?

You two haven't got laid in so long that you believed her over me."

"We..." Freddie hangs his head. Good fucking riddance. "We fucked up, and..." He looks pained. "We need your help to make it right."

I consider his offer, putting my hands behind my head. "What's in it for me?"

"He's unbelievable," Seb gripes. "Now I'm having second thoughts about whether we need him."

Freddie raises his eyebrows. "You'd be part of the team again."

"How do I know I can trust you?" I challenge.

"The feeling is mutual," Seb mutters. "You're the one who kept Rose's identity to yourself."

"I had my reasons," I say defensively.

"And that reason is now buried six feet underground," Freddie says. "You need us, Callen. You don't want to admit it, but you've got used to being a Duke and part of our family."

I weigh my options. I don't hold grudges, and working alone has its challenges. That, and I can't get into the Killers Club's base without help…

"Fine." I grin, and swivel around and stretch my legs to rest them on the coffee table to annoy Freddie further. I turn to Seb. "Did you miss me, sunshine?"

"Fuck you," Seb says, but his tone is light.

Freddie grins and shakes his head. "Welcome home, Callen."

I wink at Seb, hoping to get a bigger rise out of him. "You can't get rid of me."

"But there is one condition to your return," Freddie says. "You tell us everything you know, and no more lies."

I snort. "You're the one who let Rose blind you with her tight snatch."

For a second, Freddie's calm exterior drops to give me a glimpse of the raging monster within. But his anger isn't for me. It's for her. He strolls over and holds out his hand. I stand, staggering slightly—whatever I was drugged with is still in my system—and grasp his hand.

"The Dukes are a family," Freddie says. "We stick together. If we don't have trust, we have nothing, and we won't be making the same mistake again."

I swallow and nod. His grip is firm, crushing my fingers, filled with a promise and drive for justice. Now that he's lost the doting puppy-dog look, I can respect him as my boss again… well, for as long as it suits me.

"So, we need to fill you in on what we've discovered," Freddie begins.

# CHAPTER 38

IVY

I must have drifted off. I didn't think sleeping would be possible, but I managed it somehow. I wake up and find my head resting against Bram's bare, inked chest with his arm wrapped around my shoulder, holding me close like he doesn't want to let go. Considering the circumstances and lack of cushions, his muscled pecs act as a decent warm pillow, providing a barrier from the damp brick wall. He notices me stir. My eyelids feel heavier than usual, and I sit up, wipe them and then tilt my neck from side to side to get out the kinks.

I'm exhausted. We only have two water bottles left and no food. I'd kill to have beans on toast right now. The lack of natural light means we can't tell what time of day it is, and don't get me started on going to the toilet and the zero privacy. Thankfully, Bram always turns away when I use the wretched hole in the floor, but having to use drawing paper to wipe almost gave my clit a paper cut.

"We have to get out," I croak. Even the glow from last night's intense orgasm doesn't erase the bleakness of our situation. We have to act fast before we lose all our energy. "I'm—we're—not dying in here."

Bram stays quiet, sporting a stoic, easy-going expression, like he's lost in a meditative trance and lusting over an imaginary breakfast.

"There has to be an escape route," I say desperately, racking my brain to think of anything Alaric might have told me about the cells in the past. Although HQ was my home for a while, I never spent much time in this part of the building and only encountered prisoners in the torture chamber. "A loose brick could open the door." I think of all the tricks I've seen in films, clutching at hope. "Or a hidden key. Something like the fireplace in the Dukes' man cave."

He arches one eyebrow. *So you found the hidden room?*

"What do you take me for?" I scowl. "An amateur?"

I get up to my feet and stretch. My muscles scream for me to sit down and conserve strength, but we have no time to waste. Bram jumps up. One of his giant hands wraps around my waist while he slaps the other over my mouth.

"Hey!" I object, my voice muffled, but he presses his hand tighter over my lips.

I'm about to bite him when I hear it…

Voices approach.

"What do you mean, he's still alive?" Stephanie's voice floats down the corridor towards us. I recognise her angry tone. A low rumble from Alaric follows her outcry, but they're too far away for me to understand what he's saying.

Bram removes his hand and backs away. He catches my eye and puts a finger to his lips.

No shit, I mouth.

We don't move an inch, straining to overhear, when a door slams against the dungeon wall. We move to opposite sides of the cell instinctively. They can't learn what happened between us last night. If they weren't questioning my loyalty already, screwing a prisoner would definitely be enough to put me in a coffin.

Stephanie's heels echo off the stone floor as she nears. She opens the hatch on the door, and a waft of her familiar sweet perfume hits me. A smell that used to be a sign of comfort sends a shiver of fear down my spine because her eyes narrow when she sees both of us still breathing.

"You're both still alive. How disappointing." I can't believe this is the same woman that I poured my heart out to over the years. "Alaric won't be happy."

Am I nothing more than a worker to her? Did those years mean *nothing*? We shared secrets, partied, and killed together. While no one could replace Daisy, she was an ally.

"Stephanie!" I jump up. There's no sign of Alaric yet. "How long are you going to keep me here?" I try to channel my usual sassy self. "Locking me up with a prisoner might be your best prank yet, but a girl has to pee in peace."

"This isn't personal, Ivy. You know what you have to do to free yourself," Stephanie replies, glancing away. I detect a hint of regret in her voice, but that vanishes when she continues. "Alaric already made that clear." Her gaze strays to the water bottles. "If you don't kill each other, you'll die of dehydration first."

I glower at her, wanting to yank off her perfectly applied fake eyelashes and wrap her blonde locks around her neck. "If you won't let me out, why are you here?"

"I need something from you," she says. "I need you to make a phone call."

I cross my arms and laugh. "I'll only make the call from the other side of this door."

"I have water," she bargains. "Six litres of it. If you make the call, you can have that, and I'll bring food too. It'll keep you going until you kill him."

I avoid looking at Bram for fear of what Stephanie will see on my face when I do. We're trained to read people, so I try to keep my expression blank.

"Killing him is illogical," I say. "We'd lose our bargaining chip with the Dukes."

"Alaric makes the rules, and we follow them," she replies like a brainwashed cult member. "Now, do you want the supplies or not?"

I don't have a choice. I need to buy more time to figure this shit out. She has the upper hand and knows it. If I refuse, she'll only come back tomorrow with less food, and we'll be thirsty enough to agree to anything.

"Prove it," I challenge. She reaches down to grab a bottle of water and holds it for me to see through the hatch. "I want half the supplies before I make the call."

She pouts. "I thought we trusted each other."

"So did I," I snap. The only thing I'd trust Stephanie to do right now is kill me, but I'm not backing down. "That's my condition. Take it or leave it."

"Fine." Her blue eyes sparkle, enjoying the challenge. Stephanie relishes watching others suffer, although I thought she only reserved that for the clients. It's good we never had matching best friend bracelets. "Half first, half after."

"Deal."

She passes the supplies through the opening. They

could have laced them with poison. That'd be a better way to die than having my skull bashed in by a silent giant.

"That's my part of the bargain." She holds out a phone for me to take. "Now it's your turn." She points a gun at my head through the gap with her other hand. Bitch. "You know what'll happen if you try anything."

"What do you need me to do?" I demand.

"You're going to call Sebastian Montgomery and ask him to meet you."

# CHAPTER 39

## SEB

vy…" Callen whispers her name like a dirty secret on his lips. "That suits her." He grins. "She looks like an Ivy. Hot, dirty, and deadly."

"Shut up, Callen," I snap. My defensiveness rises to the surface to shut him down. Even though I can't condone all her lies and question how much of our relationship was real, I won't let him talk about any woman like a piece of meat. "Is that all you have to say?"

Between the three of us, we pieced together the truth about Rose… or what we think it is, anyway. She's a Killers Club assassin who was planning to kill us as part of a mission, using us to get to Spencer, or both. What I can't work out is why we're still alive.

Callen rubs his beard thoughtfully, considering my question. It's more scraggly than when we last saw each other at the cottage. "Do you think she gets all her targets' dicks wet?"

Blood rushes to my cheeks in anger. "You're twisted."

Callen grins. "Don't tell me you weren't thinking it too."

I thought my connection with Rose—I mean, Ivy—was real. She's the first woman I've been interested in for years. Being interested in her has proven why I'm better off alone. She may not have wanted me for my title, but she still had a hidden agenda.

"Now isn't the time, Callen," Freddie steps in, a warning hidden behind his deep voice.

"There is something else I should tell you," Callen says. He pauses and sips loudly on his third cup of tea of the day, adding another reason to my list of why I should punch the smug bastard's face. "When Seb went on his hot date—"

"Fuck you," I snarl.

Freddie waves his hands to shut me up.

"I saw Killer Barbie leave the restaurant you were at," Callen says.

Freddie frowns, his shoulders tensing. "Killer Barbie?"

"The pretty blonde I had in a headlock the last time we had the pleasure of meeting Ivy's friends," he confirms.

"Bethany…" I murmur under my breath, knowing who he's talking about instantly. As the designated driver, I missed most of the altercation and didn't see the Killers Club. The woman Callen describes matches the description of Ivy's 'friend' perfectly. If I had seen Bethany—or whatever her real name is—at the restaurant, I would have made the connection sooner and worked out who Rose was. "I've met her before and thought she was Ro—Ivy's —flatmate. I saw her again at the restaurant when I was with Beatrice."

"You and Horse Face would make a perfect couple," Callen chips in.

"We swapped the soup," I murmur. They both look at

me like I've gone mad. "She must have put something in it. Beatrice had to leave early because she was ill."

"Save your concern over why your date was cut short," Callen dismisses. "I followed Blondie."

Freddie adjusts his collar, hanging onto Callen's every word. He doesn't say it, but his expression conveys that he still feels guilty about missing my call that night.

"I know where the Killers Club is," Callen says. "Well, one of their locations, anyway. I've been watching them. I've not seen our red-headed minx, though I've seen Barbie and the boss. If Bram and Ivy are anywhere, that's where we should start searching."

"What are we doing sitting around?" I jump out of my chair like someone's electro-shocked my balls. Thoughts of freeing Bram race through my mind. "We need to save Bram!"

"Easy does it, sport," Callen says. "Do you think we can just burst into a house filled with killers?"

"Callen's right," Freddie agrees.

I scowl. "So we're going to sit around and do nothing, waiting for Bram to die, if he isn't already dead?"

"I didn't say that." Freddie's fists clench at his sides. "Nevertheless, we need a plan to get inside. They'll have security. We can't just knock on their door."

My ringtone breaks the tense silence, the phone almost vibrating off the table. If it's my mother again, I will…

"You better get that. It could be your new wife," Callen teases.

I frown at the screen. "It's an unknown number."

"Probably a scammer," Callen says, but I ignore him and follow my instincts. It could be important.

"Hello?"

Then I hear her voice.

Hearing it is like having a bucket of ice water thrown over my head, making my chest constrict.

She sounds the same. I can still remember the breathy moans on her lips, and how good she sounded screaming my name. Except, she's not the woman I thought I knew. She's a liar.

"Seb," Ivy says. "It's me."

# CHAPTER 40

IVY

try to stop my voice from shaking.

"Rose," Seb replies. His voice rasps through the tinny speakers of the phone. "Where are you? I've been worried sick."

Stephanie gives me a pointed glare, indicating for me to hurry up and get to the point. If I deviate, she'll fill my body with bullets quicker than she'll let a mark shoot her up with cum. I know Stephanie enough to know she's not bluffing.

"Rose?" Seb asks again. "Are you still there?"

Hearing his voice makes my knees weak. His voice is full of concern, and he sounds desperate, full of hope. On our first date, I didn't know the secret he was hiding. Why did he have to be a Duke? Our relationship would never have worked around my job, but everything could have been different.

Bram's hulking presence looms behind me. I don't need to see him to feel the desperate energy coming from him. His need to be reunited with the men he sees as family.

"Bethany gave me your number," I say.

"Are you okay?" he asks. "We've been looking everywhere for you. Just tell me you're safe."

"I'm..." My voice trails off, and I swallow, fighting the urge to tell him where to find us. If I did, I'd be dead before he got into his limousine. "Yes, I'm safe."

Stephanie waves her gun to chide me along like a murderous musical conductor.

"I know what Callen did," Seb says. "He should never have made you do that. We know it's not your fault, and you didn't know what you were doing." Little does he know, I exacted Callen's revenge willingly and felt zero remorse for the pile of bodies left behind. "He's left the Dukes now. You don't have to worry about him any longer."

He and Freddie see the best in me. They don't know the *real* me. When I met Seb and reunited with Freddie, I knew I was living a pipe dream. I should have killed them both before I started to care about what might happen to them...

"We need to talk," I say. Stephanie nods in encouragement. "Can we meet?"

"Yes," Seb says eagerly. "Give me a time and a place, and I'll be there."

"I..." I stammer. "I'll text you later."

"Okay," Seb says. "And Rose?"

"Yes?"

"You know we'll do anything to protect you, don't you?" he says, making my icy heart melt. How would he react if he learned the truth? Would he be willing to save me, then? "The Dukes protect those they love."

I open my mouth, words threatening to spill from my lips about where to find us, but Stephanie snatches the phone from my fingers. She hangs up, leaving a deadly silence.

"I'll take it from here," she says.

"Hey!" I yell as she turns to leave. "What about the rest of the supplies? We had a deal!"

"You'll get them later," she replies. "After we've killed Sebastian Montgomery."

Dread twists in my stomach.

"You bitch!" I scream.

She laughs. "Is that the best you've got?"

"What would Alaric do if he ever found out how many men you have slept with before you killed them?" I sneer, hitting her below the belt. "Does he know about your little kink?"

Her furious stare burns into me like an inferno; only I don't shy away from her. She doesn't scare me. I've got nothing left to lose.

"This is why you're here, Ivy," she counters. "You've lost sight of who you are. We trained you to be a loyal killer, and now? You're not one of us, not anymore."

She storms away. Provoking her won't help, although knowing I rattled her is satisfying.

After the door slams, Bram comes to my aid, putting his arm protectively around my waist, reminding me I'm not alone.

What kind of people have I surrounded myself with for all these years? I knew they were killers, but I thought they cared about me. They gave me a purpose and a reason to live, even though they've left me to die like a mark.

Or are they right? Am I the problem? Have the Dukes fucked me up so much that my judgement is now clouded? Right now, they are the only ones who seem to care about what happens to me.

Bram is here, Seb wants to see me again, and Freddie dismissed Callen from the Dukes because of what he thinks he did to me. I may not be part of the Killers Club, but maybe I've found another reason to fight…

# CHAPTER 41
## FREDDIE

Adrenaline rushes through my veins, and I finally dare to exhale when Seb ends the call.

Callen lets out a low whistle. "She has big, hairy bollocks on her."

"So, what do we do?" Seb looks to me for guidance. He tries to mask it; Seb is more sensitive than he lets on. Hurt is written all over his face, and the sting of betrayal dulls his green eyes. His upbringing has made it hard to trust people, and he finally thought he'd met a woman interested in more than a royal title. Unfortunately for him, it was his other title she was interested in.

"We can use a meeting to our advantage," I say, glancing at the photograph in the middle of our board. Her face. The face of the woman who lied to me from the moment she told me her name.

*Ivy.*

Callen's right—the name suits her. Ivy climbs up buildings, choking and suffocating the bricks until they crumble. She encroached on my heart, strangling it and draining my energy. I've wasted years pining over a woman who never existed.

Her voice, curves, and gorgeous wide eyes are imprinted on my soul. However, like the ivy that covers buildings in pretty green leaves, she sunk her claws into all of us and rocked our foundations.

When I saw the woman of my dreams again, I thought my prayers had been answered, and I'd been reunited with an angel. Only she was toxic. Poison. She made her way into my bloodstream, holding my heart hostage, and almost destroyed the Dukes in the process. We need to cut her out… forever.

"It'll be a trap," I announce, stating what everyone is already thinking.

"This gives us an opportunity," Callen agrees.

I nod. The bittersweet reunion I imagined with her running into my arms is a fairytale. All the tenderness I once felt towards her is replaced by a blistering fury to unleash destruction.

"She's texted a location," Seb says, holding up his phone. "The Royal Duchess Hotel."

My heart stops. It's as if she wants to taunt me. I stayed at the Royal Duchess the night she went missing five years ago. I spent hours lying awake in that hotel, waiting for a call that never came. Another cruel trick and a way to manipulate me further, but I won't fall for it again.

"We can't blow this," I reply bluntly, pushing my emotions aside. "This might be our last chance to find Bram."

Callen clears his throat. I know he's about to remind us that Bram could already be dead, but we have to find out what happened to him.

"Don't," I warn Callen.

Bram is one of us, part of our family, and I'm not giving up on him yet. Besides, I suspected the Killers Club would have delivered his body to us if Bram was dead.

"Are we really doing this?" Seb looks at his phone in disgust, pushing through his pain.

He's had his heart broken, too. Welcome to the fucking club. Ivy Penrose has cut open our chests and torn out our hearts, but I won't give her a chance to stop them from beating.

"Yes. Remember, she doesn't know that we know who she is," I point out. "It could be a trap or another way for her to get information. She might not know Spencer fired us, and she still wants him dead."

Seb nods sharply. "Let's find a way to bring Bram home."

# CHAPTER 42

## BRAM

"Fucking idiot. Think, Ive, think!" She mentally lashes herself. "Why did I think she would follow through with our deal?"

I shrug and twist open the cap of a bottle of water. I take a small sip. My dry throat welcomes the liquid, but we need to ration it for as long as possible. I've survived a drought in a desert; we can survive a cell in London.

I nudge Ivy's calf as she walks by and hold up the bottle for her to take. She scowls and dismisses me. I grunt. *You have to drink.*

"Fine!" She snatches it from my fingers, takes the tiniest sip, and swills it around her mouth for dramatic effect. "Happy now?" She shakes her head, returning to giving herself a hard time. "I should have known better, but I didn't think she'd do that."

*You've bought us more time.* I shrug. For another few days, at least...

"They're going to kill Seb and Freddie," she says.

I can't allow myself to think about them—not now, because I'll break and give up. Seb and Freddie can fight.

They're always armed. They'll be fine, won't they? Still, without Callen, they're at a disadvantage.

"They're going to die because of me," she murmurs. Her face falls, and she slumps down the wall like all the fierce energy has been snuffed out of her. Ivy may have led them into a trap, but she had no choice. She picked survival. Freddie and Seb would have made the same choice. "It's my fault."

For the first time since my being here, she seems fragile. I can't allow her fire to be extinguished. I need to relight those flames if we're going to get through this.

I punch her gently on the shoulder to get her attention.

"What was that for?" she snaps, massaging the spot.

I write a message:

*You did what you had to do.*

"Will you still say that when your friends die trying to protect me?" Her eyes brim with regret. "Do you want to know what's worse than dying of starvation?" Her lips purse into a narrow line. "Dying knowing he—Spencer—is still alive. How can he be allowed to live after what he did?" Her small hands curl into fists tightly enough for her knuckles to turn white. "It's not fucking fair!"

She needs to let her frustration out and work through the process.

"You feel guilty about giving me this life, but none of this is on you," she admits. "You brought me to Alaric, but I had a choice too. He gave me two options: live a normal life or join them and get revenge. The decision was easy. I chose a life of killing because I couldn't live without her. Because I wanted to make people hurt as much as I did. I knew it would lead to death, but I would bring them—Spencer and the men that hurt her—down to hell with me."

I stroke her cheek. Her skin seems to vibrate under my caress. This is the real Ivy Penrose, the girl I rescued from the car wreckage. The one hiding beneath the death and horror. Giving her a second chance at life was my redemption, and I won't let her down now.

"I'm not like you, Seb, or Freddie," Ivy says. "I'm twisted like Callen, and I've… enjoyed the last five years. Killing people wasn't just a job. It's been my life and purpose. What does that make me?"

Someone fucked up and in need of help.

I hastily write:

*That used to be me too.*

"That's different. You were in the army," she dismisses. "You were fighting for your country and following orders."

*Is that so different from what you've been doing?*

"Freddie and Seb look at me like I'm perfect and could do no wrong, but they don't see the real me. They want to live a fucking fairytale, and…"

She bites her lip, scared to continue.

*Go on.* I wrap her hair around my finger. *You can tell me.*

"Maybe a part of me wanted to live in that world for a little while," Ivy whispers. "Being around them showed me what life could have been like if Spencer hadn't destroyed my entire world."

I tip her chin upward and kiss her forehead tenderly. This isn't the end. It can't be, not like this...

This time, I'm not saving Ivy from a jealous ex-boyfriend; I'm saving her from herself.

# CHAPTER 43

## SEB

So far, everything is going to plan. I've been waiting at the bar on the ground floor of the Royal Duchess for hours. Ivy has a habit of arriving early, and we're not taking any chances this time.

As a team, we had to choose who was going where. While I was adamant about heading to the Killers Club base, Freddie insisted I go to the meeting location to meet Ivy in order to keep the act going. Meeting an assassin alone isn't ideal, so I have a trick up my sleeve…

As if by magic, the paparazzi appear outside the hotel, pointing their cameras in my direction. It's the first time I've been happy to see the vultures. I'm not heading into a trap without the chance to document every second.

*Good luck trying to kill me in front of the nation, Killers Club.*

I drain my pint. The booze doesn't numb the strange prickling sensation across my skin that I've had since learning the truth about Ivy. How could I have been stupid enough to fall for a woman who wanted to kill me?

I loosen my tie. The bulletproof vest underneath my suit is extremely uncomfortable, yet I can't be too careful.

"Any sign of her yet?" Freddie's voice comes through my microscopic earpiece.

Although I'm not at the Killers Club location, I'll hear everything that goes down in real-time. I pick up my phone to make answering more inconspicuous.

"Nothing," I reply. "You?"

"Nothi—" Freddie cuts off.

"What is it?" I ask, gripping my glass tighter and scanning the room for anything unusual. "What's happening?"

A group of women look in my direction, giggling and whispering behind their hands. They know who I am, but are they secretly Killers Club agents, too? Everyone I look at now falls under suspicion. After being tricked once, how could I ever trust anyone again?

"Two people are leaving," Freddie says. "The blonde and the boss. No sign of Ivy."

"Interesting," I ponder.

There's still time for Ivy to meet me unless her cronies are coming in her place.

"They're getting into the car," Freddie says. "You'll be able to track it from your phone."

Callen planted trackers under every car on the street earlier today. It won't be long until the Killers Club finds it, but hopefully long enough for us to monitor their movements in the present.

"Aw, looks like there's trouble in paradise," Callen says. "They're arguing from the looks of it. The big guy looks like he needs to bust a nut."

Freddie hisses something in the background. I can't hear what he's saying, though I reckon he's telling Callen to stay focused. Everyone knows not to mess with a wasp's nest, and they're heading straight into a swarm.

"It's approximately a twenty-minute drive for them to get to you in current traffic, Seb," Freddie says.

"They're cutting it fine," I say. "I'm starting to feel like I'm being stood up."

"That'd be a change, pretty boy," Callen teases.

"Keep us updated," Freddie says. "Remember, Ivy might be coming from somewhere else."

"Don't worry, boss," I say. "I've got everything covered."

"We'll see you on the other side," Callen says. I picture him bouncing with excitement. He gets hyped up during any job when there is a prospect of violence.

They need to make sure Ivy's colleagues are far enough away before they break into the house. If other agents are on the inside, anything could greet them when they blast open the door…

# CHAPTER 44

## CALLEN

"How much longer?" I whinge, as each second drags on.

I crack my neck from side to side, making the bones click. I want to start smashing shit.

"One minute," Freddie says, checking the map on his phone. Barbie and her Ken-gone-bad look like they're heading in Seb's direction. "Do you have everything ready?"

The device is good to go. It's another homemade creation that'll blast through the door with no problem and is detonated by a button from a distance. Bram would be proud of my technical prowess. This was our best shot of getting around the retina scanner with our limited time and lack of supplies.

"All systems in place," I confirm.

Freddie checks his Rolex and nods. "It's time."

I step out of our car in a postman's uniform. I had to knock out a poor schmuck doing his rounds a few streets over. The lucky fucker will wake up in one of my favourite jackets, so it seems like a fair trade.

My hair is tied in a bun, hidden under a cap, and I pull the visor lower to shield my eyes. Nosey neighbours won't look twice when I approach.

I hang my head while I climb the steps to the house and place the parcel carefully on the ground. I can't hear any noise from inside, although I'm sure the walls are sound-proofed.

Two cameras positioned above the door point in my direction, and I reach into my pocket to grab a can of black spray paint. I spray indiscriminately, hoping I've covered the surface of the cameras. We don't care about concealing our identities, but we want to make sure anyone watching from a distance can't see what's happening live.

"Hurry," Freddie encourages through the earpiece. "You're no Banksy, and you're certainly no Raptor."

I scoff at the mention of the mysterious unidentified artist. "Maybe I could be Wanksy."

I snicker as I grab my crotch, even though Freddie can't see my motion. Jokes aside, Freddie's right. The Killers Club would get notifications of movement outside their front door. I open the cardboard box and turn my attention to the real job. I take the device out carefully and secure it to the door handle.

"Done."

"Get back," Freddie hisses. "The coast is clear."

I return to the pavement and check again for pedestrians, mostly for Freddie's benefit. I don't care if someone gets caught in the crossfire, but Mr Holier Than Thou would never let me hear the end of it.

"Ready," I confirm. "Let's light this baby up."

I press the button.

*BANG!*

It happens in slow motion, unfolding like an action

scene from a film. It's not as beautiful as watching Lord McGowan being blasted into pieces, but it's a pretty sight, nonetheless.

After the explosion, the door remains in its frame and teeters on its hinges. It'll be easy enough to smash it open using brute force now.

"Real subtle," Freddie says, clapping me on the back. "The police will be on their way soon."

"Not that soon," I reply smugly. "I made a call to my brother. He owes me a favour. The Met is having technical faults and is behind on their calls."

Freddie's lips purse. He doesn't like us working with my brother, even though having an evil twin can come in handy sometimes.

"Nice," Seb comments from the abyss. "I'm leaving now. The two agents are closing in, and there's no sign of Ivy. Good luck."

"I'm not just a pretty face." I grin. "See you soon."

Freddie charges forward. "Let's go."

We climb the steps. I expected us to be met with a wall of ammunition, except for the fact it's ghostly quiet when we reach the destroyed door. What's going on? This is supposed to be an assassin's base, not an old people's home.

Freddie and I exchange a confused look. He's thinking the same thing I am.

"Let's not count our chickens just yet," I say.

We use our combined strength to pry the door open enough to slip through the crack.

"Not too shabby." I whistle, looking around the empty hallway with its fancy floors and chandelier. I remove a gun from my waistband. "Where's the fun in this?"

Freddie ignores me, putting on his heat detection

glasses and looking up to scan the upper floors. We have to use every tool in our arsenal with time against us.

"No one's here." He frowns, walking forward. His gaze lingers on the long bookcase at the end of the hall. "There's something behind there."

"Oh, goodie," I declare. "We all like a secret door."

Freddie removes his glasses and heads to it. He runs his hands along the books carefully. Screw that! I swipe my arm across the shelves to knock everything from it and throw the first editions to the floor.

The bookcase groans in agreement and slides to reveal an elevator.

I bow at Freddie smugly, acting like a true gent. "After you."

"We're going underground, Seb," Freddie says. "We might lose signal."

# CHAPTER 45
## FREDDIE

"How is anyone meant to know where to go?" Callen grumbles. He looks at the unnumbered buttons and decides to press them all. "We need to get one of these lifts, boss."

Seb talking in my ear fades to a crackle when the lift whirs into life as we travel into the unknown and then comes to an abrupt halt. I gear myself up for what's waiting. So far, this has been easy. Too easy. As the door opens, Callen's still talking about his dream supervillain cave and not paying attention.

That's when I see it.

Suddenly, I lunge and knock Callen out of the way of a bullet. "Look out!"

He needs to watch where he's going. The bullet streaks past him and narrowly misses his ear. Instead of being perturbed, a giant smile lights up his face.

"Here comes the cavalry," he declares, drawing his gun and shaking his long hair loose. It tumbles down and sits around his shoulders like a Viking warrior. "Let's fucking go."

We step out of the lift into an office. The beige room has a lingering mildew smell and uncomfortably low ceilings. The only splash of colour comes from a grand-looking cat palace with pink, fluffy cushions in the corner. Seemingly, the cat has better conditions than whoever works here.

Bullets continue to fire in our direction. They're coming from behind a large filing cabinet, and the barrel juts around the side of it, masking our view of the shooter. Their bullets come in a confused and random stream. Whoever is firing has little skill. Narrowly missing Callen must have been a stroke of dumb luck. They're not shooting to kill; they're shooting out of fear.

"Save your bullets," I tell Callen.

We're not wasting our ammo when we don't need to. I advance, and Callen covers me from behind in case it's an ambush. It isn't difficult to avoid bullets when they're being fired here, there, and everywhere with no aim. The printer seems to have taken the brunt of the feeble attack.

As we get closer, I hear the gun click. They need to reload. I point my gun as we move around the cabinet and come face-to-face with a frizzy-haired woman with over-sized glasses kneeling on the floor.

"Don't shoot!" she begs as desperate tears fill her eyes.

She squeaks as Callen raises his weapon and closes her eyes, but I hold my arm out to stop him. She can't talk if she's dead.

"Where are you keeping Bram Deveraux?" I demand.

"I..." Her voice shakes, and snot drips down her face. "I... I don't know."

"We don't have time for this," I snarl, aiming my gun at her head.

"Okay, okay!" She holds up her hands. "He's in the dungeon!"

"Take us there," I order.

Callen grabs her by the shirt and forces her to her feet. He roughly pats her down to check for weapons, then hooks his arm around her neck.

"You make a good human shield," he hisses menacingly. "Now lead the way, and don't think about taking us on a wild goose chase, or I won't think twice about twisting your head off your shoulders."

# CHAPTER 46

IVY

All of Bram's muscles tighten. He reminds me of a guard dog whose ears prick up at any sign of danger.

"What is it?" My chapped lips make it painfully difficult to talk, and I move off his pillowed chest to stare up at him. We haven't moved from our spot on the floor for hours, and the heat from Bram's embrace is the only reminder I'm still alive. "What's wrong?"

He puts a finger to his lips.

I listen, but nothing… then… something faint in the distance.

"You heard that too, right?" I ask.

He nods and rises to his feet.

"It's probably nothing," I say glumly, not bothering to move.

I've already resigned myself to dying here. They have no use for an agent they can't trust. Killing Bram will achieve nothing when they'll kill me regardless. Besides, I guess Bram isn't so bad after all…

We listen intently for more noise, even as the silence stretches on.

"See? I told you, we're not getting out of here," I say. "There's no—"

Fuck! Another sound this time, only it's closer. I recognise it. The sound of bullets bouncing off the walls. We have a soundproof shooting range on-site, and Alaric would never permit shooting indoors for the risk of ruining his precious decor.

"Something's wrong."

I stand now, adrenaline giving me an extra burst of energy. I don't know whether we should stay quiet or scream for help. My heart slams as Bram shoves me behind him.

"I can take care of myself," I huff and shove past him. "And, sorry to break it to you, but muscles don't stop bullets."

A low rumble comes from the back of his throat in warning. He stands at my side, clenching his fists.

A few minutes pass with nothing, and then we hear the elevator door open. There's a female voice, but it's not Stephanie. What's Penelope doing here? She rarely leaves her hiding spot unless… someone forced her.

"Bram?" a familiar voice yells. His voice bounces off the brick, making everything around me fade away until it's all I can hear. "Bram?"

My vision swims.

It's him.

Freddie.

He's here.

Bram races to the door and pounds against it, signalling where we are.

"We're coming," Freddie calls. The hatch window pops

open. He can't see me hiding behind Bram's enormous frame, and I'm too stunned to speak.

My body responds involuntarily to his voice. A swell of hope consumes my chest quickly, followed by a crushing realisation. If he's here, what does he know?

"Fuck!" a raspy Scottish voice swears. "We need a combination to open it."

Callen's with him? Seb said on the phone that he left the Dukes. I inhale deeply, pushing aside the vulnerable Ivy whom Bram's got to know and bringing out the ruthless killer to the surface. If Seb lied to me on the phone, he must know who I am… and who I've been working for. I have to be ready to fight.

"What is it?" Freddie asks. "Put in the code."

"I…" Penelope stammers in response. "I don't know it."

Bram knocks to get his attention, then holds up his fingers in sequence to let him know the numbers. Thankfully, Alaric hadn't changed it back already.

Callen types it in. With a satisfying click, the door swings open, but this isn't the freedom I expected.

Freddie's imposing figure stands in the doorway. As usual, he's impeccably dressed and hasn't broken a sweat. His pale blue shirt is rolled up around his elbows, and the top buttons have fallen open to reveal his tanned skin. Even when he's taking a risk by breaking into an assassin's house, he looks like he's stepped straight out of the pages of a magazine.

Next to him, Callen's blue eyes glint menacingly. He's wearing a short-sleeved shirt with a postal logo printed on the front paired with three-quarter-length shorts, the opposite of his usual rugged biker look. His beard and hair have grown longer, giving the impression he's been sleeping rough for weeks. In his tatted arms, Penelope whimpers in a headlock, looking to me for help.

I step from behind Bram and growl, "Let her go."

Freddie's gaze sweeps across the cell and lands on me. His jaw hardens, looking me up and down, and his lip curls in disapproval. He looks straight through me like I'm a total stranger. The man who cared for me and spent a night focused entirely on my pleasure has vanished. An icy statue stands in his place. I don't recognise this man.

Callen laughs coldly, tightening his grip on Penelope until her face turns purple.

"Would you like to swap places, princess?" Callen challenges.

And unlike Freddie, Callen hasn't changed at all.

# CHAPTER 47

## CALLEN

There she is.

*My princess.*

She steps from behind Bram like a phoenix rising from the ashes. Her skin is ghostly pale with a translucent quality, accentuating the redness of her hair, and her eyes are ringed with a bluish hue.

Bram looks like he's done rounds in a boxing ring. He's shirtless with new scars, wearing torn trousers, and has a bloody piece of fabric wrapped around his thigh. Although he's still a giant beast, he's lost weight—so maybe now I stand a chance of beating him in an arm wrestle.

"Don't hurt her, Callen," Ivy says. "She's not an agent."

What gives her the right to think she can bargain with me? I'll murder this wriggling Killers Club scum in my arms just to prove a point.

"And how do you expect us to believe a word you say, Ivy?" Freddie counters coldly.

Ivy recoils when he speaks, flinching like she's stepped

out in a snowstorm. Poor princess isn't getting the royal treatment anymore. She needs to be put in her place.

"You don't have to believe me," Ivy replies, refusing to back down like the stubborn, no-shit-taking bitch I know she is. Man, she's hot. "But I know you don't want to kill innocent people. That's not what the Dukes stand for."

I scoff. "Don't pretend that you know us."

"Fine." She shoots a look of pure hatred in my direction that makes my cock stir, reminding me of the first time we fucked. "Do you want to stand around arguing some more or get the fuck out of here? If we don't leave soon, we'll all be dead."

I glance at Freddie for approval, cocking my head to the side. He nods curtly. I smash Penelope on the side of her head with the butt of my gun—it'll make her dizzy for a few days, but it wasn't hard enough to cause a severe injury. She slumps to the ground, unconscious, at my feet.

"I never said you were coming with us," Freddie says. "We're not here to rescue you. We came for Bram."

Suddenly, Bram slips his hand into Ivy's. Freddie's eyes rest on their interlocked fingers, and a vein twitches in his forehead. Freddie's gaze scorches into Bram, who stares straight back. Bram can't speak, but his stance is clear. He won't leave without her.

"It looks like you've ticked another Duke off your list," I goad her. "Did you think there was a prize for fucking the full set? Our cocks aren't bingo numbers."

Bram growls and tightens his grip on her. *She comes with us.*

"We need to go," Ivy presses. "They'll know you're here already, and whether you admit it or not, I'm the best chance you have at getting out alive."

"And you expect us to trust you?" Freddie asks. His

voice is thick with sarcasm. "How do we know you're not leading us into another trap?"

Bram tenses and shakes his head.

I've never seen him so worked up before. What did Ivy do to capture him under her spell in the cell? His time in captivity has finally made him grow a pair of balls... and get laid. I've heard about his time in the army, but maybe this experience will draw him out from behind his keyboard again.

"It's a risk you'll have to take," Ivy says.

"Not unless we kill you first..."

# CHAPTER 48
## FREDDIE

want to leave her locked up in this hellhole, alongside my feelings for her. However, Ivy's right. She is the best chance we have at getting out, and from the look of Bram's injury, he needs to see a doctor immediately.

"No one's killing anyone," I say through gritted teeth, tempering Callen's murderous rage. "If you even think about crossing us—"

"We don't have time for this conversation," she bites, stepping out of the cell and tugging Bram after her. "We need to move."

She pushes past me. I step over the woman's unconscious body and hope we haven't made a mistake by leaving a witness behind.

"Fuck," Callen says. "Do you hear that?"

The lift is being summoned to another floor.

"Come on!" Ivy calls, breaking into a run.

Bram limps along after her like a lost puppy. When we get out, we'll help him through whatever form of Stockholm syndrome he's going through.

Ivy takes us through the maze of corridors and up a

few staircases. I only get a quick glance at the rooms we pass but see weapons and training areas. Begrudgingly, I have to admit this is one of the best operations I've ever seen.

"This way!"

She leads us to a heavy-duty silver door and turns the handle. My gun is already out, pointed at her head as she pushes the door open. She pauses, feeling the weapon pointing at her through an innate sixth sense, and turns to look at me. She raises her eyebrows. "Really?"

"You can't be too careful," I seethe.

She continues into an underground garage where rows of cars are waiting. There's everything from sports cars to bullet-proof jeeps.

"Joy riding," Callen comments. "Nice."

"Just hurry up and pick a fucking car," she growls. "The keys are already in the ignition."

My anger surges at her authoritative tone. Who does she think she is? This is our mission. We're here to rescue Bram, and she's tagging along for a free ride because she's fallen out of favour with her friends. Clearly, she upset the Killers Club to be locked up like a prisoner, unless it's another act.

When we first met, I wanted to wrap my arms around her and take her to bed, desperate to hear her moan my name and draw every last drop of pleasure from her. Now I want to wrap my arms around her pretty throat and make her beg for my forgiveness.

Suddenly, a male voice comes from behind us as I open the door of a sleek, black Land Rover.

"Stop!"

I spin to see him pointing his gun at Callen.

He has a distinct scar over his neck, and wires dangle out of his arms like he's broken out of a hospital.

Callen smirks, rising to his bait, and pulls out his gun just as fast. "Are you always this welcoming to your guests?"

"Don't!" Ivy jumps in front of Callen to stand between them in the line of fire. I don't know who she's trying to protect. "Jonathon—just let us go, okay?"

Jonathon's eyes narrow into bloodthirsty slits. "You know I can't do that."

He aims for her head and shoots. So much for loyalty. The bullet hurtles through the air, and Bram springs into action. He dives forward to push her out of the way, and the bullet plunges into his bare chest.

No… he can't…

Ivy's scream makes the hairs on my arms stand on end, and I let rip a roar, acting before Callen has the chance. I empty my rounds into Bram's attacker with no mercy. I keep going even after he falls to the ground. No more second chances.

Meanwhile, Bram staggers on his feet, holding onto the bonnet of a nearby car for balance. He sways for a few seconds and drops. Ivy crawls across the ground from where she landed to his side.

She pulls his head onto her lap, cradling him in her hands. This was supposed to be a rescue mission. We found him alive. We can't lose him at the last hurdle.

Bram's chest heaves, his breathing growing ragged. They share a meaningful look, but whatever she sees on his face angers her.

"No!" she screams. Desperate tears fill her eyes, but she refuses to let them fall. "You've saved me once before; now it's my turn to save you."

# AUTHORS NOTE

Thank you to Kyla and Ria, my beta reading babes, for being keen-eyed and giving me so much encouragement along the way.

Thank you also to all my readers who are coming along on this journey with me. This series has been giving me emotional whiplash, so I hope you're recovering too! You're the best, and I appreciate you more than you could know.

# ABOUT THE AUTHOR

Holly Bloom has a degree in English Literature, but don't let that fool you... she would pick a steamy romance over a Shakespeare play any day!

Holly writes contemporary romance - the dark, gritty and twisty kind. She loves creating badass babe characters, who aren't afraid to speak their minds, and writing about the men who can handle them - often, there is more than one! Why choose, right?

When she isn't working on her next project, Holly spends an unhealthy amount of time watching true crime and roaming around the woods near her home in the UK.

As well as gooey chocolate brownies, Holly's favourite thing in the world is hearing from her readers - her characters may bite, but she doesn't! Promise!

**Find out more and sign up to Holly Bloom's newsletter to receive a free book at:**
**www.hollybloomauthor.com**